With a vision that transcends the normal and a value system nurtured by his love for both tradition and modernity, Gourahari has been able to see and comprehend the nature of conflict and complexities of a society in transition. He has keen eyes of observation and the sensibility of an enviable creative writer.

Ruskin Bond
Ivy Cottage, Landour Cantt.
Mussoorie

With its feminist perspective, this novel has its thrust on the marginalization of women, her bold confrontation with hostile forces, an assertion of personal freedom, and her triumph over oppressive male-oriented societal practices and prejudices. This is the story of a woman's crusade for her emancipation from the same biases, injustice, and tyranny.

Prof. J.N. Patnaik
Professor of English and Eminent Critique

The Dawn After the Long Night is a revolutionary and path-breaking creation in Odiya literature. Every chapter of it creates a yearning in the mind of the reader.

Prof. Bhagabat Behera
Poet and Critique

Dawn After the Long Night

Gourahari Das

Translated by
Tapan K Panda

Black Eagle Books
2021

Black Eagle Books
USA address:
7464 Wisdom Lane
Dublin, OH 43016

India address:
E/312, Trident Galaxy, Kalinga Nagar,
Bhubaneswar-751003, Odisha, India

E-mail: info@blackeaglebooks.org
Website: www.blackeaglebooks.org

First International Edition Published by
Black Eagle Books, 2021

DAWN AFTER THE LONG NIGHT
by **Gourahari Das**
Translated **by Tapan K Panda**

Cover: **Tanuj Mallik**
Interior Design: Ezy's Publication

ISBN- 978-1-64560-234-7 (Paperback)
Library of Congress Control Number: 2021951421

Printed in the United States of America

Dedicated To
The Woman
And
Her Fighting Spirit

Author's Note

The essence of *Dawn After the Long Night* is that when life throws us hundreds of reasons to lament, we need to show hundred-one reasons to laugh – or else we will be unable to live this life. Along with this, there exists another significant truth -There exists extraordinariness within every ordinary person. Peculiar life situations pull out that extraordinariness.

On its first release in Odisha, this novel created ripples among readers. This novel was and continues to be a reassuring exception in the tradition of depicting a helpless and lamenting female protagonist. I firmly believe that the English version will reach a wider audience and touch the sensibilities of non- Odiya readers across the globe. In this direction effort of Dr. Tapan K. Panda, a distinguished writer and trans-creator, is praiseworthy. My warm wishes to him for completing the trans-creation of this novel into English during such a short period.

I hope the readers will be able to explore the identity of an Indian woman through her adoring love for values, tradition, her struggle, and soul-searching inquisitiveness in this novel. I also congratulate Sri Satya Patnaik, publisher, and Mr. Ashok Parida, the creative head of The Black Eagle Books, on releasing this book.

Gourahari Das

Anubhav
378 Baramunda Village
Bhubaneswar- 751003, India
9th October 2021

Dawn after the Long Night-
The Saga of Hope

Out of suffering have emerged the strongest souls; the most massive characters are seared with scars –Khalil Gibran.

This is the message of this novel. Suffering is part of everyone's life, but if that is meant for a woman, it increases many times for no reason that can be attributed to the soul. So then, what drives life? How come some people come victorious from this eternal struggle? This novel 'Dawn after the Long Night' (Eithu Arambah) brings this message to its readers.

This novel is unique in many ways. The novelist Sri Gourahari Das- a master craftsman of his genre, has left no stone untouched in building a storyline that gives us hope, encourages us to face challenges and vagaries of life with boldface- only to win at the end. Along with this, he is also a commentator of the socio-political history of modern Odisha. In his novel, at multiple times, he has thrown hard-hitting questions to readers to ponder over, to think through. This novel is a classic piece that pushes the reader to awaken his soul. The message is direct and gut-wrenching.

The novel portrays the struggle of a woman who didn't give up despite all the difficulties in life. Urbashi, the protagonist of the story, is a bold character and sets an example for the other women in society to fight back despite all odds. The novel depicts the pain, suffering, and agony that a woman goes through when rejected by her near and dear ones. This is where we learn a lesson. Pain is to be expected, courage to be welcomed, and no choice but to endure. There is no other way than to renounce self-doubt. In this male-dominated society, fighting back and surviving is an arduous task, but nothing is impossible when you get the support of a companion like Pulak. You will never feel alone when you run down the stairs of loneliness and have a faithful companion.

The novelist has evolved over the years as a writer but has built his unique style to build characters, sketch the obvious, and is a master craftsman in his way. The power of his words is always stronger than his persona. I have always seen him as a very soft person who speaks with measured words. But when he picks his pen, he is someone different. His musings are about ordinary people, their suffering and his writing always ends with a message of hope and possibilities. I am a loyal reader of Sri Das, who decided to trans-create this novel for English readers.

This is my seventh translated novel but one of the most exciting works I have done in the recent past. I am thankful to Sri Gourahari Das for permitting me to translate this novel for a wider audience. I strongly feel that Odiya literature should reach a larger global audience – that is one of the missions of my foundation- Tapasya Foundation. I have experienced a similar passion with Sri Satya Patnaik at Black Eagle Books (BEB). My sincere thanks to him for partnering with Tapsya Foundation on this mission. I also thank Mr. Ashok Parida for his contribution in bringing the pieces together into such a beautiful book.

Tapan K Panda
Hyderabad

Preface

Someone rightly said that there is always a beginning before the ending. The end of a city may be the beginning of a village. The end of a trail may be the beginning of a wood, plateau, or desert. An estuary begins where the river ends. Maybe the sorrow ends with happiness, or the joy ends with misery. If you look at the ending as the beginning and the beginning as the ending, then there is no end, and there is no beginning. We come across such things in life. When we think that we have reached the dead-end of life and there is nothing left, a miracle happens, and in the darkness, there is a canopy of shadow, and life inside a soul never fails to peep through. A spark, a flicker, holds on to that tunnel of hope.

'Dawn After The Long Night' is a smile on the lips of melancholy. When I began writing the novel, I didn't have an idea about its ending. In my 'Chayasoudhara Abasesha' (The Fading Rainbow) novel, I thought of writing the novel based on the past or flashback, but after writing a few pages, I felt as if the story's protagonist questioned me,' Who gave you the liberty to portray me in this way?' I was startled and remembered that it's a human tendency to become happy at others' sadness. We represent the woman as delicate and fragile, and do we get happiness out of it? One can write stories in two ways for a female protagonist. Firstly, what is the audience's view of the actress on the stage, and secondly, how does the actress look at the audience? When it came to my mind that the way Urbashi looked at society and the view of society about her was different, I tore the pages and began from scratch. The next thing which worried me was time. I couldn't get an opportunity to take a break from the monotonous life and devote my time to writing. I understand that people praise the people who succeed in life, and they don't have time to listen to the worries of an unsuccessful person. The readers are more critical for a writer, so who will he narrate his story other than them?

It's my honor that for this novel, I received many accolades. Many writers congratulated me on this. Critics say that in my novels, the women always go through unhappiness and ill fate but never bow down in front of uncertainty. In the novel 'Chhayasoudhara Abasesha', Minu doesn't regret it when she sacrifices her life. In the novel' Nija Sangae Nija Ladhai,' the character, after becoming fearless, stepped out, but Urbashi's life was different from theirs. Urbashi is a character of the past and the future. The character justifies the values in life but also knows how to tackle the worst.

After reading the novel, the readers gave their opinion about the relationship between Urbashi and Pulak. The Editor of 'Kadambari' asked me why will not the relationship between them proceeded further? Few of them had the opinion that they should get married. Some of them said, why can't it be discovered that Pulak is Nilamadhaba? It's not that I didn't think about these possibilities. I remembered a sentence said by Pulak,' There is no definition for our relationship. The association is confined when a name like father, son, husband, or lover is given. Beyond these definitions, relationship exists.' For this, many readers have thought of me as a heartless writer. I can't deny this. I am responsible for it. After reading 'Ahalyara Bahaghara,' one of the readers wrote a letter to me in anger and said that to gain name and fame as a writer, I have made girls like Ahalaya cry.

I remember a few incidents when this novel was first published. One of these is very precious to me. A young Sanskrit teacher in Kendrapada was reciting Gita in 'Sambada's office. I am not fascinated by the way the brahmin chant mantras, but this young man fascinated me. He chanted the slokas from the chapter 'Vishwarupa Darshan' in such a way that I was amazed, and after that, I decided to quote two slokas of Gita in my novel. One more incident related to my wife Sanjukta, who is a writer and a translator. She inspires me with her comments. After completing the manuscript of the novel, she wanted to listen to it. If no one is there to listen to the manuscript, then it isn't easy to make out whether it's good or not. A writer can never evaluate his write-up as a child always looks beautiful to his mother. On that day, Sanjukta sat with me till midnight to listen to the manuscript. After reading it, I could see tears in her eyes, and I felt that my efforts didn't go in vain. What can be more valuable for a writer?

I have already narrated many things which weren't required. My dear readers, this is an opportunity to convey a few things. I hope that the readers will like the novel, and if that happens then, my efforts will not go in vain.

- Gourahari Das

'Anubhab'
378.Baramunda village
Bhubaneswar -751003
Odisha, India

CHAPTER 1

CAPITAL

Urbashi was sitting on the oil-stained bench on the porch of the main office of the opposition party. Bharat Mahapatra, the journalist, made her sit there for a long time and went inside, but he didn't return. She was disgusted with the roving eyes of the passer-by and long hours of sitting. When she looked at their eyes, she felt as if those people did not see a woman for a long time. She could even hear them discussing about her in a feeble voice. They were discussing among themselves,' She is Urbashi Pattnaik, who lodged a defamation case against the Minister of Environment and Forest. She is the wife of Rourkela's ruling party leader Sanjay Pattnaik. Yes, the lady who became insane. Have you not seen her photograph in the newspaper?'

Urbashi wanted to pull her vanity bag from her left shoulder to hide her face. Do all the people in the state know about her? Is she insane in the eyes of others - She asked herself. The commoners know in detail about her; maybe the President of the opposition party too knows of it and doesn't want to meet her. Why is Bharat Mahapatra taking so much time? How long will she stand on the porch and listen to the gossip and mockery of the passers by? She is the one who has experienced it and knows how difficult it is to spend every single second. She had a notion that the opposition party leader would listen to a helpless woman's plight and meet her at least once. She may not get benefitted from it but will find solace. But now, she apprehended that her meeting with the President wasn't possible.

Urbashi's acquaintance with Voice of India's journalist Bharat Mahapatra was adventitious. No, not precisely adventitious because after a theft case how the investigation of the police isn't adventitious -in a similar way, her acquaintance with Bharat Mahapatra isn't adventitious. Till she was confined to the four walls of the house, her acquaintance with police, lawyer, journalist, or politician wasn't required. At that time, her priority was her family, home, husband, and in-laws. She didn't need to have any relationship with the outside world, but those were the stories of the old times. When she looks back, she feels as if those were the stories of her previous birth or someone else's past. Otherwise, why won't there be any correlation between the present memory and history?

Urbashi had been waiting for a long time, and now she was feeling very thirsty, but she didn't want to drink water from the water bottle. Maybe after drinking water, she might feel like going to the washroom, and there is no ladies' washroom nearby. It is the main office of such a big political party; many renowned political leaders visit this place, they discuss the future of the state, but they couldn't think about this minimal requirement. She was unhappy about it.

Urbashi once again looked at her wristwatch. The reporter Bharat Mahapatra promised her that he would try to make it possible for her to meet the opposition party President on that day. He told her to wait for only five minutes, but now it's almost two hours, and there is no sign of Bharat Mahapatra. Whatever she heard about the journalists is not false. Bharat Mahapatra has forgotten about her and must discuss his interest with the opposition party President. He might have taken some amount from others for their transfer or posting. It has come to her knowledge that few journalists in the capital do this type of work. For the transfer of a doctor or engineer, they get in thousands. If one could get one or two jobs done by a minister, fifty such works can be done quickly from all other ministers together in a year. Other than that, spending the evening in a club or a star hotel comes as a bonus that's why there is a lot of competition among the youth to become a journalist in an itty-bitty newspaper. Urbashi had heard that the ministers keep the renowned journalists under their grip. Is Bharat Mahapatra that type of journalist? If not so, then why is he taking so much time?

Jagannathpur College's lecturer Rabi Das introduced her to Bharat Mahapatra. He wrote a letter. Rabi Das was the English lecturer in the college where Urbashi worked for a few days after completing her MA. After Urbashi gave her resignation, Rabi Das joined in her post. At that time, the college secretary, Mr. Murari, advised her not to resign from her position. At present, when she recollects what Mr. Murari said, she becomes remorseful. But that day, why would she have expected such a situation?

She remembered what the lecturer Rabi Das said. For the first time when Rabi Das saw Urbashi on the college campus, he was baffled. Urbashi laughed, looking at Rabi Das's facial expression despite her grief. On that day, she realized that a person who doesn't have anything isn't the unhappiest; instead, a person who lives with the apprehension of losing a little of his possession is the most disappointed. Rabi Das had the same expression when he saw Urbashi as if she would snatch away his job. Rabi Das was old enough to get a new job; other than that, it was difficult to get a new position in the present situation irrespective of the age factor. One lakh people will be employed within five years because of the election manifestation that the government has already forgotten. Instead, the government sacked hundreds of government employees. In this situation, when Rabi Das saw Urbashi, he was surprised. It was pretty natural. But there was a similarity between Rabi Das and Urbashi. Both of them had lost faith in God and the government. Whatever faith was left, that was on one's self.

Bharat Mahapatra was coming towards her. Urbashi looked at him and took a deep breath. They reached the place at 10 am10 am, and now it's 12.17 pm12.17 pm. She stood up hurriedly, and the umbrella which was kept on her vanity bag fell. People who were around her looked at her when they heard the sound. Urbashi didn't pay any attention to it. She asked very curiously,' What happened'?

Bharat Mahapatra said,' let's go outside and discuss this. Today you can't meet him.'

Urbashi was dejected. She waited for a long time and was very tired, but there was a ray of hope which was her strength. During that time, she recollected her past experiences and memories and felt uncomfortable, but still in that distress, she saw the light at the end of the tunnel. She envisioned, even though she was in so much sadness, humiliation, remorse, and regret, burning like a flame amidst the storm.

She followed Bharat Mahapatra and went down the staircase. Before Bharat Mahapatra could say anything, she asked him if she was interrogating him,' What were you doing there for such a long time?'

Bharat Mahapatra felt a little bit uneasy. He was also a little scared. He had met the lady hardly fifteen days back. Before that, he had read in the newspaper regarding Urbashi but had never met her personally. Now when he heard the shrill voice and looked at the annoyed face of Urbashi, he was bewildered. Is this lady insane? He stepped back a little, apprehending that Urbashi may harm him. He thought she might scratch him with her nail, pull his hair, or may pull his collar. If it happens, then he can't show his face to anyone. People in his profession will poke fun at him, and others will have a negative impression.

He had read in the newspaper an article featuring Urbashi. Urbashi's in law's left her in a hospital in Ranchi, Bihar. They told her that when she recovers, they would bring her back from there. After two years, when Urbashi recovered completely, her husband didn't go to get her back. The doctors in the hospital wrote letters to them mentioning,' The patient has already recovered and is eager to return home. People come here to recover from their mental illness, but ordinary people don't need to stay among the mentally sick people. You may go and take her....' But neither anyone from her in law's side nor her near and dear one's came to take her. If the Human Rights Commission wouldn't have interfered, then Urbashi still would have been there. That's why Bharat, who was sympathetic towards her, was willing to help her. But Bharat Mahapatra didn't know whether Urbashi had recovered entirely or not.

Bharat didn't know if his friend Rabi Das to help Urbashi or to shift his responsibility on him, wrote a letter to him. When Bharat heard from Urbashi regarding the matter related to the teaching job, he thought, maybe to be free from the guilt conscience, Rabi Das wrote such a letter to him as he hardly knew Urbashi.

It happens like this. Here the best way to carry out one's responsibility is to entrust it to someone else and be free from all the worries. Sometimes for courtesy's sake, you need to ask that person,' How far is he through with the work?' to ask this, it's not necessary to go to that person personally. It can be done through the exchange of letters or phone calls.

'The President was sleeping.' Bharat replied.

'Sleeping?' Urbashi stood there surprisingly.

'That's why I was late. The gentleman is old enough. He dozes wherever he sits and then falls asleep. I was in his PA's room waiting for him to wake up.

'But, I have been sitting on this bench for the past two hours. Urabashi said in a firm voice. You could have come and told me the same thing!'- She said.

'What I could have done? Was it possible for me to sit like you on the bench or enter the Chairman's room?'- He said. That's why ….

'You sat in his Private Secretary's room! Right!' Urbashi completed Bharat Mahapatra's incomplete sentence.

Bharat didn't answer anything.

Urbashi kept quiet for a moment. She shouldn't have

expected so much from Bharat Mahapatra. She said,' Leave it, I am ill-fated. Why will I blame you unnecessarily?' Urbashi's fair face turned red while saying this.

'No, No, why are you thinking in that way? This place isn't always crowded. Sometimes this opposition party office is deserted. Other than the election work, what else is the work in the political party office? Of course, there is a crowd in the ruling party's office, but this opposition party is a regional party. All the decisions are taken here, and the President is the main person who takes the decisions. He is also a little bit irritating type of person, that's why most of them don't dare to meet him. Even Sarangi babu….

'Sarangi babu?'

'His Private Secretary.'

'Oh! I thought you were saying something regarding Dr. Sarangi.'

'Who is he?' Bharat asked.

'Psychiatrist. Leave that matter. What will I do now? What did the President say?' Urbashi asked.

Bharat said,' Look! To speak truthfully and frankly, I wasn't taken aback by his answer.' Then he again said,' He knows everything in detail about you. It means he has heard about you, and he can't take the risk to make you a contestant. He paused…

'Why don't you say it clearly? You may speak. You needn't be worried about how I would feel. Just think that I don't have any feelings. I am like a machine. I will listen through one ear and discard through the other. I won't have any reaction.'

'NO, no, don't become so sentimental. He didn't say 'no.' His party's Political Consortium Committee will decide over it.'- Bharat said.

'But just now, you were saying that the President is the all in all of the party. Others don't speak in front of him. Is it so that he wants to say 'No' through his Political Consortium Committee?'- Urbashi asked in a straightforward way.

The journalist Bharat Mahapatra was surprised to listen to Urbashi's question. He is a journalist by profession. His job is to question others and make them suffocated by asking question after question to articulate the enigma. His job isn't to answer others' questions; that's the work of others. But Urbashi Pattanaik is asking him questions and expects him to answer, but he cannot answer.

Maybe for the first time, Bharat Mahapatra realized that it's complicated to answer the questions. It's a difficult task to respond to rather than a question. It's even more challenging to answer general questions rather than unknown questions.

Bharat Mahapatra is an experienced journalist. He has undergone training at Delhi for journalism. He has a good grip on English, that's why he has chosen his career to be a journalist for an English newspaper. The Odiya newspaper owners don't pay well, and other than that, there are so many restrictions. All of them speak about principles but do the reverse. Most of the owners of the newspaper want to become the Chief Minister. They aren't happy with their identity as the newspaper owner, and their employees have to bear the tantrums of their discontent. Before joining 'Voice of India,' Bharat Mahapatra worked for an Odiya newspaper for some time. He didn't like the owner's displeasure and less salary paid to him, so he tried a lot and finally joined an English newspaper. There is suitable regard for the English newspaper in Odisha. In the meetings, people hue and cry for their mother tongue, but in reality, they don't give importance to their mother tongue.

Many ministers and higher officials even don't read an Odiya newspaper. Whoever goes to other states like Calcutta, Hyderabad, or Surat for a job, their language is Bengali, Telugu, or Gujarati. For those who are well placed, their spoken language is English. Odiya as a spoken language is limited to the villages and farmers. That's why when someone gives a speech in Odiya though it's not well articulated, people clap. The journalists who work for an English newspaper are respected more in the capital than the Odiya newspaper journalists. People think that they don't get into dirty regional politics. If a statement is published in the English newspaper, then the party high command staying at Delhi doesn't get the Odiya news translated into English. That's the reason why the politicians give more importance to journalists of English newspapers.

Bharat Mahapatra is happy with his status, and his happiness is justified. Now he has noticed that rather than newspaper journalists, TV journalists are more acclaimed. All of them are behind them. There is no authenticity left in the newspaper news. Once upon a time, the court had also accepted a report published in the newspaper as the public petition. But that isn't the situation at present. The reliability of the newspaper is declining day by day. The journalists bring into light the same news in different ways. That's the reason why the court isn't giving attention to the reports published in the newspaper. If Bharat Mahapatra gets a chance, he will switch over to TV media. Till that time, he has to work as the representative of 'Voice of India' Bhubaneswar to keep his identity intact.

Till then, Urbashi didn't get an answer to her question. To make Bharat Mahapatra realize that, she coughed to draw his attention.

Bharat Mahapatra was now out of his thoughts and looked at Urbashi. The anger reflected on her face doesn't suit her appearance. Her unkempt hair had covered her face. She was sweating. He wanted to change the topic, so he looked for a trivial reason to appreciate Urbashi's beauty. Suddenly he remembered that just a few days back, Urbashi was mentally ill. If he tries to be informal and crack jokes with her, maybe he has to pay for it. He said,' The word 'Hurry' isn't the trend in politics.'

'I couldn't understand what you said, said Urbashi.

'I have already put a word to him. It will take some time for him to understand it.'

But Rabi babu was saying that you have an excellent rapport with the President. During the election campaign, he took you along with him on the flight. Along with the editor of your newspaper the Chairman has ....

Though Bharat Mahapatra showed a gesture of being uncomfortable, he was feeling happy from within. He was enjoying the appreciation by Urbashi. Like Urbashi, the other people who stay far from the capital also know about his reputation; this isn't a small matter. His association with the President is a topic of discussion among the other journalists in the capital. But, the people who are away from the capital also know about it, he liked this.

Bharat said,' When he was in power, he took me along with him three or four times. That's not a big issue. The desk journalists have already visited the United States of America and England. I think you know very well that desk journalists are like animals with sharp teeth and claws. What respect I could earn in comparison to them?'

Urbashi was annoyed. She said,' I didn't ask you about your prestige.'

'Oh! I am sorry. I was a little bit distracted. Maybe Rabi has praised me a lot in front of you. He is a literature student, so he has the habit of exaggerating things. He must have also overstated my relationship with the President. Other than that, the President isn't in power at present. Why will he need me? We also publish the statement of the opposition party President; otherwise, people will think that we favor the ruling party.'- Said Bharat Mahapatra.

Urbashi didn't answer anything. Bharat Mahapatra's way of talking made her feel hopeless. But Rabi Das told her that Bharat Mahapatra would do her work.

Is Bharat Mahapatra expecting something from her? But, what does she have? She doesn't have money. She is spending her life like a helpless person depending on the sympathy of others. What can she give to Bharat Mahapatra? How can she entertain him in an expensive restaurant or a club? She doesn't have that capability. She took a deep breath and said hopelessly,' I may leave now. I have taken a lot of your precious time. Kindly excuse me for that.'

'Oh! No, No. Why are you thinking that way? But don't lose your hope. Call me back after a few days. If there is any development in this matter, I will let you know.'

'But you haven't given me your phone number. Rabi babu told me about your quarter number, so I reached there.'

'Ok, you may take.', Bharat Mahapatra said. He took out a visiting card from his wallet and gave it to Urbashi. He said,' The visiting card has my phone number and address. You may contact me between 10 pm10 pm and before 10 am.'

Urbashi folded her hands.

Bharat Mahapatra started his car. He waved at Urbashi and went outside the gate of the opposition party office.

The sun was shining brightly in the afternoon. Urbashi looked around. There was an intersection of roads. On the right side was the hospital, on the left side was the AG square, on the backside was the government quarters, and on the front was Forest Park. Four roads were leading to different directions. One has the option to select any one of these four roads. But which route would Urbashi select?

CHAPTER 2

NUAGAO

On her way from the capital to Cuttack, she remembered about her village Nuagao. Six years back, she went to Nuagao for the last time. She couldn't visit during her father's death. Maybe she wasn't allowed to go, or no one required her presence, or she didn't want to go. She doesn't want to remember those old tales. If she tries to remember it then it will give her pain. By the time she reached Nuagao, her father was dead. But why did she go to Nuagao?

Her village was on the shore of the Bay of Bengal, far away from the capital. She was born and brought up there along with two sisters and two brothers and got a little bit of love and affection during her childhood.

Yes, a little bit of love and affection because she was an unexpected child for her father. After two daughters and two sons were born, her father didn't want any more children. She was the fifth child and was a girl. As soon as her father came to about her birth, he said,' It would have been better if the child would have died.'

Urbashi laughed at herself. As soon as she was born, she was cursed; then why did she take birth? She is still alive, and is it not more painful than death?

The road looked green with the greenery in the paddy field on both sides in that August afternoon. Her village fields are full of vegetation, and the egrets sit there quietly searching for the fish. The tall palm trees look like guardians from a distance. Among all these, Urbashi remembered her last visit to the village and her bitter experience. She doesn't know why all the known faces looked unknown; all the known sights looked unseen as soon as she reached the Nuagao square.

The bus plying between Bhadrak and Dhamara left her as if she were a discarded paper packet. Urbashi lifted her bag and looked around cautiously. She felt as if all of them had become alert after her arrival, and all of them were conspiring against her. People who were there left their work and looked at her. They said the Girl had become insane. Someone said she is trying to defame and blackmail the elite people by giving statements in print against them. Someone also said the wealthy father is responsible for spoiling the Girl.

Urbashi couldn't tolerate this. Though she has heard these things from others, she never expected it from her people in the village. She believed that it doesn't matter what people speak about her, but the people of her town will trust her because they are like her extended family members. They will never leave her behind.

She took away her hands which had covered her ears.

She couldn't hear any noise. The small marketplace was a little bit crowded and noisy. Is it so that what she heard was the creation of her imagination? For the first time, her unassertiveness solaced her rather than giving her discontent. Let the delusion remain. She can never accept the reality that the people of Nuagao are heartless and insensitive.

Urbashi looked around in search of a rickshaw. It was scorching, and she was carrying a heavy bag, so she couldn't walk to her house. She saw a rickshaw and called,' Hey! Rickshaw.' The rickshaw didn't stop and moved ahead.

Urabshi was shattered. Does the rickshaw puller know about her? Is it because of that he didn't want to give her a ride? No, no it can't be so. Then what can be the reason? Why didn't the rickshaw puller stop though she called him? The rickshaw puller wasn't so far that he couldn't hear her. Then ….?

Urbashi unnecessarily doubted the rickshaw puller. In reality, there was no fault of the rickshaw puller because Urbashi didn't call him. She was reluctant to speak. She never wanted others should see or hear her or know about her presence. She wanted to go away from there being unnoticed. She tried to hide like an ant in the anthill.

The old rickshaw puller was standing before her for a long time, but Urbashi didn't notice him. Later, as she saw, she kept her bag on the rickshaw and said,' Mohanty Sahi.'

The old rickshaw puller dragged the rickshaw for some time and then sat on the seat. The rickshaw was rolling down on the slope. Urbashi was looking on both sides of the road through the slit on the hood. She came across the school playground, the Shiva temple, the canopy of the goddess, and the same known road leading to her house, but she felt as if all these were new to her.

In between the market and the village on the left side

was the Nuagao High School and on the backside was a vast playground. Urbashi felt restless when she saw that ground. She looked at the garden. The ground was barren as the grass didn't grow. Once upon a time, she played ring ball, volleyball, football and ran on that ground, but time flies. Urbashi was the front player of the Girl's football team. Many boys came to see her playing, and girls encouraged her by clapping as she played.

Urbashi felt as if her fate was like the fate of the football rolling on the playground. On that day, a few children were playing football on the ground. A boy was holding the ball under his feet and talking to someone. In a while, the ball will roll, and the game will begin.

The life of a ball in the ground! A ball rolling on the floor doesn't have its independence. The helpless and frightful ball keeps on moving from one end to the other end, from one corner to the other corner, sometimes high up in the air and sometimes crossing the boundary. Still, the enthusiastic spectators and players clap with delight, and the ground resounds with laughter and joy. The ball neither wins nor loses; it's only kicked from here to there. It keeps on rolling as if it's sacred, shaky, and wants to save its life. This is the fate and destiny of a ball.

Urbashi's eyes were filled with tears. Is her fate different from the fate of a ball? She is also like a ball going through the turmoil in life. Like the reaction of the ball, her response is also ignored by others.

Urbashi made herself comfortable to meet the family members. She had never thought that she had to come back to Nuagao again. She could have returned long back if she had deemed, but how could she return? How could she face her siblings? What would she have complained against her in-laws? Will they trust her words? Could she tell them that she has left everything behind and has come back? What would she have told her neighbors and others?

That day she came back to the village without anyone's invitation. As she was nearing the house, she was losing her confidence. In that darkness, her spirit has doled out. She remembered the story that she read during her childhood about the magic ash. If she could get that magic ash, she could smear it on her body and become invisible for years together. No one can see or perceive her. She wished she could become thin air and hide forever in the shrill music of Kendra(A wooden string instrument), in the reflective prayer, and in the scent of the grass so that no one will look for her, ask for her or discuss her.

As soon as she reached the house, she became listless. She took some time to climb the stairs. Her home was the biggest in Nuagao's Mohanty Sahi. The flooring of the courtyard was red, there were many rooms, and the main door was too big. Urbashi stepped into the house slowly.

Her elder sister-in-law was draped in a tussar saree with a red border, held a brass plate with different flowers on it, and returned after offering her prayers. She looked gorgeous. Urbashi bent down to touch her feet. Her sister-in-law moved back a little and said,' Today is Lakshmi Puja. Go and take your bath.'

Urbashi thought that her sister-in-law could have politely said the same thing. She and her sister-in-law were almost of the same age, and as she was married to her elder brother, she respected her. Her sister-in-law isn't much educated. She got married many years after Urbashi's birth, but she is the house owner, whereas Urbashi is just a house's daughter. Urbashi was an English lecturer, but she didn't mean anything to anyone in the house.

Her elder sister-in-law was performing the Lakshmi Puja. This puja is performed on Suklapakhya Dasami and a Thursday. Women perform the puja to be blessed with good fortune and wealth. They tie a thread on their arm, which has ten knots. Urbashi took a deep breath. She thought the ladies who are blessed perform this puja, whereas she is jinxed. How can she perform it?

She controlled her feelings and emotions and entered the house. Her younger brother was about to leave for the market. He ignored her and went away. She was standing in the mid of the courtyard and was thinking where to go. Her brothers were staying separately in the same house after the death of her father. The courtyard and the room where her mother stayed were commonplace in the house. Her mother had her food in turns in both her brothers' places.

She was in pain at the callous attitude of her brothers and sister-in-laws. It was more painful than the torture that she went through in her in-laws' house. She couldn't imagine how she would have reacted if she had been in their place, but she had never expected this type of behavior from them. She rather expected that her brothers would scold her, scream at her, maybe her elder brother would slap her, but none of them did anything as such nor spoke to her correctly. All of them ignored her presence as if she wasn't the daughter of the house but an unexpected guest whose presence wasn't required.

After some time, someone came and called her to

have her food, but Urbashi wasn't interested in eating. She was lying down in that darkroom of her mother.

It was almost evening. She remembered that during her childhood in the evening, her mother used to come and close the windows of her room and say,' These bloody mosquitoes will suck my daughter's blood.' She lit the incense in an earthen vessel. Urbashi doesn't remember whether the mosquitoes went away after burning the incense or not, but that irritated her. Her mother came and caressed her lovingly. She is her mother, so she could immediately perceive the touch of her mother. She turned to the other side and looked at her mother. She was looking pale and sad.

Urbashi dug her head into her mother's lap. She caressed her and said,' You are ill-fated. I don't know at what time I gave birth to you. You didn't get the happiness in your life.' Her mother couldn't say anything more and sobbed. She was trying to hide her tears and disgrace.

Urbashi didn't want to tell her mother anything as she knew that whatever she wanted to speak, her mother wouldn't be able to hear that. She wanted to say, 'Leave it, mother, don't think about my happiness. The parents forcibly took away their daughter's happiness and left her unattended then why will the outsiders think about her happiness?'

Her father's photograph was hanging on the wall with a garland around it. As no one wiped the picture, there were traces of cobwebs on it, but none thought about it. Just four months back, her father was the whole and sole of the house, and no one dared to speak in front of him, and now his photograph is covered with cobwebs. Urbashi had a lot of complaints regarding her father. Why did her father spoil her life?

Urbashi's mother slowly took her hand off her back as she could understand that her daughter was unhappy with her husband. She left Urbashi there and went for the evening prayers. Urbashi wanted to shout and call her mother like she used to do in her childhood, but she didn't call her; rather thought let her go. Why be unhappy with an old widow? Why will she be angry with the old lady who has her food in turns in her son's house despite having a lot of property?

She wanted to tell her mother that no one requires her presence as they think she is characterless, but what about her other two daughters? Why doesn't she go to them? But she couldn't ask her. She knew that her mother couldn't do this. She is an orthodox lady and thinks she shouldn't drink a glass of water in her daughter's house. She can never accept the proposal of staying in her daughters' house. She will stay at Nuagao despite all the humiliation. It's her house, her life, and the reminiscent of her husband.

Urbashi was comparing the fate of a woman with a man. Let it be Princess Diana or a girl from Nuagao like Urbashi; both are like materialistic things in this male-dominated society. Why will anyone bother about their likes and dislikes?

There was turmoil in her heart. She believed that at least in Nuagao, she would live peacefully as going back to Rourkela wasn't possible for her. Ms. Nalini of 'Sahajog' ditched her, and that moved her. If she goes back to Sanjay Pattnaik's house, maybe he will feel pity for her and at least feed her with a square meal per day but rather than that, it will be better to end her life and not live like an animal.

She was patiently waiting for her brothers' decision. She had a hope that her brothers would understand her. She has tied the rakhi in their wrists, and now in this situation, when she requires their help, they will appreciate her. But at that time, she didn't know that her sisters-in-law were making all the decisions at home. They were the whole and sole of the family and both her brothers were competing with each other to justify who is more devoted to his wife. Though the younger brother had a difference in opinion with the elder one but regarding Urbashi he was also with the decision of his elder brother. People said,' It won't be wise to keep the Girl here who couldn't stay in her in-laws' house.' When Urbashi was in the village, it was pointed out about her character. They said,' How did the girl file a defamation case against such a respectable leader? Mukund Mohanty's money has spoiled the Girl and if Urbashi will stay in the village, then the girls and women of the village will go astray.'

None of them uttered a word to support Urbashi. Her elder brother didn't say anything, as he didn't want Urbashi to stay in Nuagao as she may demand from their father's property. This feeling was like rubbing salt into wounds. She couldn't tolerate what her brothers said, her sister-in-law's callous attitude, and the helplessness of her mother. She was torn apart. It was not tears but blood dripping from her wounded soul.

It is her village where she had taken birth and had grown up. She was brought up in the air and water of the town and played in the playground. During the festivals, she visited different places along with her friends, and those people of her village have seen her growing up from a child to an adult, and despite that, they didn't show a little bit of sympathy for a fatherless girl.

Urbashi looked through the bus window, wiped her tears, and said to herself – Nuagao be away from me, that's better. As she went needless to Nuagao, she came back needless. After listening to her brothers that evening, she decided that she may die but would never return to Nuagao again.

Before the sunrise, when all of them were sleeping Urbashi took her bag and left the house. She didn't think that it was necessary to wake any of the family members. She wished she would file a case against her brothers as, like the brothers, all the sisters also have equal rights over the property, but if she does that, then her mother will suffer for the rest of her life. Near the door, her mother was standing cautiously to bid farewell to Urbashi. Urbashi's heart melted as she saw her. Her mother quickly gave her a small bag. Urbashi could guess what was there in that small bag. There were a few pieces of jewelry and some money that her mother had. Urbashi felt like throwing the bag at her mother's face and saying,' Keep your things with yourself and give it to your daughter in laws.' But if she had done that, that would have hurt the feelings of her mother. Her mother would have forced her to take, and she would have denied it; there would have been some arguments, and her sisters-in-law would have woke up from their sleep, and after that Urbashi would have left, but they would have humiliated her mother now and then which would have been more painful. Urbashi silently took the small bag from her mother's hand and left the place.

CHAPTER-3

CUTTACK

As soon as she opened the gate of 'Ashraya,' Shakuntala came and said,' Mr. Acharya came to meet you. Did you go to their party office?'

Urbashi asked,' Who is Mr. Acharya? Why is he so much interested to know where did I go?'

Shakuntala works for 'Ashraya' Working Women's Hostel. She has been working there for the past seventeen to eighteen years. At present, there are a few more Working Women's hostels in Cuttack, but at that time, it wasn't there. If she wouldn't have got a shelter there, then where would she have been? Nowadays, Shakuntala doesn't think much about her ill fate. Once she thought of herself as the most unfortunate person in the world, but slowly her misconception changed, and now she realizes that few are even in worse conditions than her. When we see a person more unhappy, we compare that person with ourselves and get the strength and courage to survive.

Shakuntala is almost fifty years old. She has experienced life in these eighteen years. She is so experienced that now she can guess about a person's nature from the body language. She said,' Mr. Acharya is a leader in the opposition party. He had been to the party office today and had seen you there.'

'Why did he come here?'

'Sometimes, few animals also step into this hostel.' Shakuntala said and laughed.

Urbashi had a headache as she waited for two hours, traveled by bus, and then the shoe store incident at Ashok Nagar made her sad and irritated. She wanted to take some rest, so she didn't want to discuss further about Mr. Acharya.

Shakuntala could read her mind and said,' Sometimes the things which can't be done- at the point of the sword can be done quickly.' Urbashi could understand the indication of Shakuntala. She sat on the bed and asked,' What does Mr. Acharya do?'

'His job is to greet others.'

'To greet! Is that a job?'

'Who said to greet others isn't a job? When Mr. Acharya came to this city when he was twenty-seven to twenty-eight years old. He studied law at Cuttack and then shifted to Bhubaneswar. Once he got an idea that he will only greet others and earn money.'

What Shakuntala said seemed to be like a puzzle to Urbashi. Urbashi said,' I can't understand what you are saying?'

Shakuntala said,' Listen! He was standing at the back gate of the Secretariat, and whoever was entering, he was greeting them. They include the Commissioner,

Secretary, Ministers, Contractors, and the Suppliers. Few of them greeted him, and few of them thought that he was welcoming them by mistake and didn't pay attention.'

'It's queer.'

'It's not queer rather intelligence. Once a person came and gave Mr. Acharya a hundred rupee note. The man was a contractor, and he was looking for an opportunity to impress the minister of his division. He was motivated by looking at the way Mr. Acharya greeted people. Tell me whether it is a big thing to be greeted as soon as you enter the Secretariat- Urbashi smiled. Shakuntala said,' After this, the man got the technique. He regularly visited the places like a guesthouse, circuit house, and Dak bungalow. He greeted people like the ministers, MLAs, and other leaders. Those along with the ministers thought that Acharya was very close to the ministers, and then the businessmen and the contractors caught hold of him to get their work done.

'That means the person is a crook? Why did he come here? Urbashi was a little irritated.

Shakuntala said in a feeble voice,' Now he isn't the same person how he was before. He is a well-known leader in the opposition party. He is very much skilled in arranging meetings, processions, and strikes. He has three to four buses and seven to eight trucks. Whatever I told you about him, it was when he began his career.'

Urbashi said, 'You may go now. If he comes again, please tell him that I am not interested in politics, and instead of bothering me, he should focus on his work.'

Shakuntala went away. Urbashi looked at Sahkuntala and thought about her future. The more she thought, the more her future looked unclear. She remembered her daughter Miki as she didn't see her for a long time. Does Miki remember or think about her?

What will she do now? After she lost the defamation case against Ramraman, she has lost her confidence. Her in-law's family and her so-called husband are celebrating her defeat. Maybe after this, she may fail in the divorce case filed by Sanjay Pattnaik. What will happen after that?

What will be her identity then? Will it be a characterless insane woman or a woman who tries to hide her own mistakes and weakness, so she conspires and defames others? Is she a woman who, without reason, tried to rob the honor of the elite group?

She doesn't have a house, a family, a husband, or a child. She doesn't have anything other than a wounded past and an unpredictable future. What will she do? Urbashi again thought of committing suicide. How will she commit suicide? If death were in her destiny, she would have died the day her father got her forcibly married to Sanjay Pattnaik. She could have died the day Sanjay Pattnaik kicked her like an animal, spitted on her, and danced hysterically. She could have passed away the day when the Forest Minister promised to help but misbehaved with her. Today there is only one reason to die, and that is her defeat. She can't get back her honor and love because of her elder brother's decision.

Urbashi wasn't able to decide. She knew that another thorn could take out a thorn, and so is politics. But who will support her candidature? The opposition party leader denied meeting her. Will she meet Mr. Acharya and discuss with him? As Shakuntala said, if a weapon can't win a war, it can be in other ways. But if he betrays her, then what will happen? She remembered her father, who was the Sarpanch of the village. He wanted to climb the ladder of success in politics. There was no limit to his ambition. He never wished to limit himself to the designation of a Sarpanch. He wanted to be an MLA or the Panchayat Samiti Chairman and to earn in lakhs. He had a dream to construct a house in the city, to have cars, and so on. There was no limit to his plans. He believed that he could achieve all these by connecting with affluent people, and that's why he chose the ruling party's youth leader Sanjay Pattnaik and got her married to him. Sanjay Pattnaik was a stepping stone to achieve his goal.

She was told that after knowing that Urbashi is in love with an unknown person, Sanjay Pattnaik is interested in marrying her, so he is an ideal young man and only people like him can set examples for others.

Sanjay and ideal? Hatred filled her heart. She closed her eyes as if a dangerous animal was standing in front of her, and she didn't want to look at it. Slowly the fear and hatred were subsiding from her mind, and the fog was becoming apparent, and in the midst of this, she could see a hazy smiling face of a man.

Where did Nilamadhaba go? He weaved her dreams and aspirations, but she didn't get a chance to meet him for once.

Urbashi remembered the good old days. She met Nilamadhaba through a pen friend column in an English newspaper. A few lines of his poem and a brief introduction about him were published there, but there was no photograph. Nilamadhaba wrote about the restrictions in human life. He had mentioned that sometimes we don't have the liberty to make the decisions in our life. A decision like where he will be born and where he will die is not taken by a person, then what's the necessity to worry about trivial things in life. He narrated his views beautifully. After reading that Urbashi was in love with him, she wrote a letter to Nilamadhaba in his Delhi address the next day. In that letter, she congratulated Nilamadhaba and also mentioned, though we cannot make major decisions in our lives, can't we decide to be friends? After a week she received a reply to her letter.

Urbashi never got so much love and affection from anyone, neither her father nor her brothers. For them, love and attraction don't have any meaning. The appreciation that she couldn't get from her family she got from an unknown person. Isn't it a fantastic coincidence?

Urbashi's life is filled with such coincidences. After that to write a letter to Nilamadhaba every week was a part of her routine. In the year 1982, Nilamadhaba was studying at Delhi University and was one year senior to her. Urbashi was studying in Vani Vihar at that time.

One day her father got a letter from Nilamadhaba, and that changed the course of her life. Urbashi doesn't know how her father got the letter, but that was the last letter from Nilamadhaba to her. She didn't have the opportunity to read the letter. Who knows what did Nilamadhaba write in that letter?

Her father said that she was born in an inauspicious time. It's unfortunate for parents to give birth to a girl like her. Urbashi was born in the year when the government revived Rourkela's Steel plant, Satyajit Ray won awards for his film Aparajita, Nagaland state came into being, and Jonna Pinto of Mumbai won the Beauty Pageant at Los Angeles but Urbashi, who was born at that time in Nuagao was an unfortunate thing for her parents.

Despite so much irreverence, why did her mother name her Urbashi? She is the only person in the world who accepts her and forgives all her mistakes. She has read about Urbashi in the Purana. In Deva Sabha, the most beautiful Urbashi attracted Pururba and was cursed by Indra to take birth in this mortal world. When Urbashi got married to Pururba, she put forth two conditions. The conditions were: Firstly, till she doesn't see Pururba naked, she will stay with him, and secondly, till the time a pair of lambs will be there near her bed, she will be his queen. One day Biswabasu stole the pair of lambs of Urbashi, and when she tried to wake the king up from sleep, she saw that the king was sleeping naked. That day she was free from the curse and went back to heaven.

There are many tales in the Purana related to Urbashi. She also fell in love with Arjuna and went to him to plead for his love. Though Arjuna appreciated the beauty of Urbashi, he rejected her. Urbashi felt insulted, and before leaving, she cursed Arjuna that he would be neutered sex and stay a few months along with the ladies. During Angyanta Basa, Arjuna disguised himself as Bruhanala in the kingdom of Virat and was the dance teacher of princess Uttara for a year. It was only because of the curse of Urbashi.

Urbash Pattnaik sometimes thinks that the beautiful Urbashi in the Purana was more fortunate than her. Here the conditions are laid by others; others give the punishment and curse. She isn't that lucky to lay conditions for others. Before she could meet Nilamadhaba, he went away from her, and as soon as she joined her job, she got married. After getting married to Sanjay Pattnaik, she became Urbashi Pattnaik rather than Urbashi Mohanty. The things took place so quickly that she didn't have the opportunity to understand and analyze, and by the time she realized, her course of life had already changed.

She had given a brief introduction about herself to the opposition party President. The reporter Bharat Mahapatra had said that he would inform her regarding it, but Urbashi didn't trust him. Maybe the opposition party President doesn't want to include a controversial woman in his party. Is it so that she became controversial and took birth as a woman according to her wish? Does society ever respect the wish of a woman? It's neither accepted in Mahabharata, Quaran, nor Socrates, Aristotle, or Manu or Parashar. A woman is worse than an animal in everyone's eyes.

While studying in Vani Vihar Urbashi took part in a debate. The topic was 'Role of Women in Hindu Culture.' On that day, after listening to her powerful speech, the teachers and students in the hall were taken aback, but today, she is taken aback by others' behaviour.

For a long time in Hinduism, the birth of a girl child was considered inauspicious. To give birth to a male child was the primary objective of marriage. The marriage of a girl and her becoming a widow was a reason to worry. Urbashi still couldn't understand whether men were born divine. A woman is required to give birth to them, but this society couldn't understand that.

Hindu society has never accepted the supremacy of a woman. Still, Sankaracharya was defeated by the wife of Mandan Mishra in logic, and Bijaya's knowledge was at par with the knowledge of Kalidas. In India, queens have taken care of the throne. The queen of Madagascar fought the battle against Alexander.

Man has written the destiny of the woman. Sometimes if a suitable groom is not found, then the Girl is married to an unworthy person irrespective of the Girl's wish. All the countries and the religion have the same view on the tyranny on the woman. Urbashi read a book by Geoffrey Chaucer while studying her MA. It was written in the book, a husband beat his wife black and blue and took her to the doctor to again beat her when she recovered. During 500 BC, men hung a whip on the bedpost to make the wife understand that she could be punished at any time. Sometimes, the Girl's father gifted this whip and other things to the son-in-law to control his daughter. But a woman always tries to protect her husband from all the problems in life. To feed the husband in prison, the mother of Ajatsatru took the risk, and Savitri fought with Yama for the life of her husband. Devi Sita entered the fire, Gandhari blindfolded herself for her entire life, and Anushya took her lustful husband on her shoulder and went to the concubine. Thousands of women jumped into the funeral pyre of their husbands. Even the most intelligent women couldn't evade the misfortune.

Neither in education nor in marriage is a woman given importance. A girl is auctioned. In her childhood, she gets married and is sent to her in-laws' place, and after the death of her husband, she follows the custom of getting married to her brother-in-law. Vyasadev in Mahabharata accepted the Niyog Vyabasta and was the reason for the birth of Dhrutastra, Pandu, and Vidura.

In the olden days, the kings had a lot of landed

property, and they gave a little of it to their soldiers for farming, but during the battle, if the soldier died, his widowed wife never got that land. The land-only belonged to the king's soldiers who fought in the war. To survive, his widow had to get married to another soldier.

King Harischandra could sell his wife, and Yudhistir could lose his wife in the dice game. In Holland, when the men couldn't pay the taxes, they gave their wives in return. The value of a woman is not more than an animal. When Urbashi remembers about those ill-fated women during the rule of Mughals, she shivers. She has read about this in the books but had never thought that her fate would land her up in this situation. Urbashi cried and wiped her tears.

CHAPTER – 4

THE CAPITAL

The President of the opposition party was sitting on the balcony of his double-storied house and was looking at the birds flying in the sky. These birds have more self-confidence than human beings, and they don't depend on others to survive. They set an example for being punctual and disciplined. The party president remembered his young days as a pilot and the thrill to fly high up in the air like a bird.

After the ruling party came to power and formed the government in Odisha, he could very well guess the cold war which was going on in his party. Those responsible for taking care of the political issues forgot their duties for their benefits and ambition. He tried his best but failed. The people he helped and gave a respectable position were now his foes and have filed a petition against him in vigilance. The base of the politics is betrayal and treachery. How can he stop this trend?

He didn't want to stay in the capital. His house, which was crowded with supporters, is now empty as not many people visit him. At present, along with the ruling party members, few members of his party were trying to defame him with the charges of having a lot of ill-gotten property and his inclination towards women. His family wasn't staying at Bhubaneswar so it was a golden chance to propagate it.

He couldn't understand what the problem is in inclining towards women? Long back, his wife had asked him a question, and he answered,' If I don't have an inclination towards women, how did I love you?'

He was looking at the branches of the old coconut tree near the boundary wall. The height of the coconut tree always inspired him. Can anyone suppress the will to climb the ladder of success? He has learned this from the coconut tree. He puffed the cigarette and left it in the ashtray.

Harekrushana Pattnaik had come to meet him. He gave a proposal to resign from the Vidhan Sabha and to contest for the Lok sabha. His proposal was good. It's better to go to Delhi rather than to be a leader of the opposition party. His family members are there to take care of him. He has been here for a long time as the opposition party leader, and he is no longer interested in holding this designation. He wanted that the younger generation should take over this responsibility.

He looked at the biodata of Urbashi Pattnaik, which the reporter Bharat Mahapatra had given him. He never had faith in the typed bio-data and the certificates. He thought that the people who don't have self-confidence carry their certificates as proof. He has sympathy for these types of people, but he doesn't support them. In the game of politics, there is no relevance of degrees, and it's meaningless. He was attracted by the name of the Girl- Urbashi.

He was engrossed in his deep thoughts. He was taken aback when his competitor Rajsekhar Mohanty became the Chief Minister without contesting in the election. Rajsekhar Mohanty is too clever. He came to know that Rajsekhar Mohanty bought the elected MLAs. The black money showed its wonders. Before the election, the MLAs who supported Sadananda supported Rajsekhar, and Rajsekhar became the Chief Minister.

The opposition party president was well versed with the shrewdness and the intelligence of Rajsekhar. Rajsekhar never invests his money before the election, but he spends money on those who have won the election. His ideal is- The value of a rising sun is more than a setting sun.

The telephone rang. He stood to receive the phone. He receives all the calls himself rather than depending on an associate. Harekrushna Pattnaik had called him to fix an appointment to meet him in the evening. He told him to meet him and disconnected the call.

The MLA of the steel city has resigned from the post of the MLA and Forest minister. His son has killed a boy by crushing him under the wheels of his jeep. The Forest Minister himself was notorious and shrewd. He didn't care for anyone as he had a lot of money. He is a strong supporter of Rajsekhar Mohanty, so though he had a vigilance case in his name, he still could become the minister. He protested this, and the ruling party said that if a vigilance case is filed against a person, that doesn't prove that he is guilty.

He wasn't much surprised to listen to the explanation of values and morals by the ruling party. There was a time when the Railway Minister resigned for a rail accident, and the ministers resigned if there was any allegation regarding their associates. But the time has changed, and now though the candidate is behind bars can still contest for the election. If any leader is convicted in the lower court, they are no longer afraid of that as they file the case in the higher court and lead a life without any worries. Although there was a vigilance case against the Forest Minster, it was still not a problem for him to be the minister.

Rajsekhar wasn't the only person to be blamed for the political situation in Odisha; he was equally responsible for it. Being in power, One can do things quickly rather than being not in control. That's the reason he remained silent though he opposed the swearing-in ceremony of the Forest Minister. Now he was giving a second thought to go to Rourkela.

The boy whom the son of the Forest Minister had killed was the son of a Dhaba owner. Around 10 o'clock, the Forest Minister's son and his friends had food and drinks in the Dhaba. When the Dhaba owners asked to pay the bill, the Forest Minister's son abused him and ransacked the Dhaba, and because of that, the dhaba owner's son pushed him. To take revenge, the minister's son and his friends tied him to the jeep, dragged him to a distance, and then killed him.

According to the instructions of Rajsekhar Mohanty, the Forest Minister took responsibility for this act and resigned. The opposition party president knew that it was a strategy to avoid the wrath of the people. If he wouldn't have left, then it would have become a burning issue. Many businessmen from the other states and were into business in Rourkela would have demanded his resignation. But he wasn't able to understand why the man was in a hurry to resign from the post of MLA. Maybe he was trying to pressurize the Chief Minister.

Harekrushna Pattnaik suggested calling for a political meeting based on this issue at Rourkela. Though he is a little bit immature, he is his strong supporter. Though others have ditched him sometimes, Harekrushna Pattnaik has never betrayed him. If he says Harekrushna Pattanik to resign from his position, he will do it immediately. Harekrushna Pattnaik is literate and knows the political economy. The only negative thing about him is that he doesn't have control over his tongue, so he has many foes, but he is a very good politician.

Rourkela's by-election will be like an attack on Rajsekhar Mohanty. In the state Vidhan Sabha, the ruling party doesn't have a two-thirds majority. Out of a hundred and forty-seven MLAs, the ruling party has eighty MLAs. Bringing down the ruling party won't be challenging if he can convince the Communist Party and other minor parties. He has to keep the issue alive till the upcoming session in Vidhan Sabha.

The morning newspapers were scattered on the table. 'OSF India' had published about the murder of the young boy on the first page of the newspaper, and other newspapers had also posted it on the front page, but he didn't give much importance to it. Chief Minister Rajsekhar Mohanty has a good rapport with the TV, radio, and newspaper reporters. He came to know that a reporter of the All India Radio had covered an issue in the ruling party office in detail, so he was transferred to Manipur. He doesn't know if it's true, but he knows very well that Rajsekhar Mohanty is very good at maintaining the personal rapport that he is lagging in. He is short-tempered - He remembered this and smiled. He doesn't exaggerate things and presents them in a polished way in front of others. The satisfaction that one can achieve from combat can't be achieved by slaying. In this state, the young people want to make easy money overnight; they aren't hard-working and devoid of self-respect, and other than that, corruption prevails.

Few of them commented that he is responsible for the increase in corruption in the state. He was the man who gifted the people with four-wheelers who didn't deserve a two-wheeler and distributed money among the people. This allegation isn't wholly false because he followed this path to pull Mahapatra down from his seat and banish him from the state's political scenario.

The party president looked at the watch hanging on the wall. Mr. Sarangi must be there in the office as it's almost eight-thirty. He meets people in his house' Tarun Tirtha' till 10 O'Clock and then goes to the party office. To call Mr. Sarangi, he pressed the bell.

CHAPTER-5

CUTTACK

Urbashi arranged the letters that she received from many and clippings of newspaper and magazine articles published about her. She also organized the clippings of the Rourkela murder case in another folder. She was surprised by the way the local newspapers printed the articles. Sometimes the reporters don't visit the scene but print the news. Other than two or three reporters, the other reporters never took any of her interviews before publishing it in the newspaper. Some even mentioned falsely that they tried to contact her but couldn't, and others didn't bother to say that. Whatever they hear, they print it without justified reasons.

Whenever Urbashi remembered about Rourkela, she was troubled by her thoughts. All her dreams and aspirations were shattered there. When she got married and went to Rourkela as a bride, she had plans in her eyes. All those got buried in the sand.

Her marriage was performed hurriedly. Her father and brothers thought that if they didn't complete the wedding immediately, she might leave the house on the pretext of appearing for an interview and elope with Nilamadhaba. If that happens, that will bring disgrace to the family.

Urbashi argued that their thoughts are baseless. She justified it by saying that eloping with Nilamadhaba is wrong as she has never seen him. She also asked if it is not the daughter's responsibility to maintain the dignity of the family? But no one trusted her words.

Till one year of her marriage, everything was going on well with Urbashi. Sometimes the memories of Nilamadhaba winked in her thoughts, but she tried to bury those memories. She knew that Nilamadhaba was her past, and the past is always past. It might be possible that one-day human beings will reach the sun, but it's impossible to go back to the past. It doesn't matter how much you try, but the past will never become the present. Nilamadhaba will never return. She had sent her wedding invitation card to the address of Nilamadhaba, but she didn't know whether it had reached him or not as she didn't receive any reply from Nilamadhaba.

One day Sanjay Pattnaik asked her many questions about Nilamadhaba. He took Urbashi to the market in his car, and near the STI square, he pointed at a piece of land enclosed with a boundary wall and said,' This is my remorse. I couldn't purchase this piece of land. I had a dream to construct a hotel here. But nearly eight years back, Sandeep Ray bought this piece of land. Whenever I take this road, I remember about this piece of land.'

To bring a change in Urbashi's mood, Sanjay Pattnaik took her to the saree and jewelry store. Most men think that a woman's need is a saree and jewelry, whereas a woman longs for loyalty. Urbashi was never interested in saree or jewelry.

In the evening, when Sanjay Pattnaik asked Urbashi why she couldn't forget Nilamadhaba, Urbashi gave him the example of the land near STI square. She said,' You can't forget a piece of land for eight years, so how do you think that I can forget my first love in a year?' The result of her straightforward answer will be malicious was beyond her expectation. On that day, she had a confrontation with the ugly personality of Sanjay Pattnaik, which had many dimensions. He pushed Urbashi on the sofa in front of her in-laws and co-sister and beat her.

The episode that began in Sanjay Pattnaik's living room on that day continued till she left her in-law's house. Sanjay Pattnaik left no stones unturned to abuse her mentally and physically. It was for the first time when Urbashi thought that she should commit suicide. Her father and brothers coaxed her for being in love with Nilamadhaba, but she gulped that poison, but now she couldn't tolerate the torture and harassment that she was going through in her in-law's house. She thought that there is no value in her life. A life that doesn't have dignity or emotions is worse than an animal's life. She didn't want to live for the sake of living. Why will she live? But she couldn't die. That evening her head was reeling, and she vomited. It was a different feeling for her. The perception which could have made her a complete woman made her uncomfortable. She kept her hand on her tummy and said,' Can someone give birth to a child in this chaos?' The fetus didn't give a reply, but she answered her question. She wiped her tears and changed her decision.

Once, someone asked her,' How was your experience being the mother of Sanjay Pattnaik's child?' The question seemed weird, but she said it doesn't matter whether the child belongs to the father or the mother after birth, but until it's in the mother's womb, it belongs to the mother.

Sanjay Pattnaik didn't allow her to live peacefully. Physical torture and humiliation had become a part of her life. Her mother-in-law and co-sister were also women, but they never opposed the behavior of Sanjay Pattnaik; instead, her mother-in-law said,' Sanjay, after knowing everything about the girl, still married her whereas the former minister Navin Patel had decided to get his sister married to Sanjay. If he had married that girl, he would have got a lot of property, and other than that, Navin Patel would have helped Sanjay achieve success in his political career. Sanjay had sabotaged his career and the family's reputation by getting married to a quarrelsome girl like Urbashi.' Urbashi was designated as a belligerent woman in a jiffy.

She couldn't understand what fun Sanjay gets by disrespecting and humiliating his wife in front of others. Why was he behaving like an insane person? Though Urbashi couldn't understand it then but now she can very well understand it. Sanjay Pattnaik's empire was built based on lies and betrayal. He had acquired the educational certificate illegally and had never respected others. He wanted to be an MLA or parliamentarian overnight, ride the costliest car and show his power over others. He wasn't concerned whether he was eligible for that or not. His father worked in the mining department as an officer and had made a lot of money by taking bribes from the mining contractors. He constructed a stately building, bought a luxury car, and spent money lavishly. The only sorrow in the life of her father in law- Sashi Bhusan Pattnaik, was his elder son Ajay who was mentally disabled.

Though his son was grown up, he behaved like a child, which had put his parents in an embarrassing situation. He spent a lot of money, consulted many doctors in this regard, took him to many saints, but nothing could be done. Sahi Bhusan Pattnaik could manage to arrange a bride for his son though he was mentally disabled. Urbashi's co-sister was from a low-income family, and she was beautiful as a doll. Urbashi appreciated her patience. Right from the morning till evening, she worked hard like a machine but was never appreciated in return. From whom she could have got the appreciation was lying on the bed like a log. Her co-sister gulped all her sorrows and worked but had no respect in the family.

After her marriage, Urbashi heard that Sanjay Pattnaik had an illicit relationship with his sister-in-law. She was surprised to hear that. Can it happen? Can a woman cross her limits just to satisfy her lust? But later on, she understood that it was the creation of Sanjay Pattnaik. He tried his best to have a relationship with his sister-in-law, but as she disapproved of it, he tried to defame his sister-in-law with the help of his party workers.

Urbashi thought that this creation of Sanjay Pattnaik was to boast that he was macho. That evening she went to her co-sister. Both of them tried to understand each other and discussed their sufferings. One of them was a sufferer as her co-sister's husband was incapable, and her husband was imprudent. They sat silently for a while, and as they became emotional, they cried and wiped each other's tears. Urbashi could very well understand the pain of her co-sister, but she didn't know how to relieve her from her sorrows. She took a deep breath and remained quiet.

Sanjay Pattnaik was shrewd and characterless, which Urbashi could ever imagine. The day she came to know about his trickery, she was taken aback. She couldn't imagine how a person who pretends to be a gentleman and a philanthropist can be so dangerous?

By that time, Miki was born, and suddenly, she came across a photograph in which a girl was dressed up like a bride. Urbashi thought it might be the photograph of one of the relatives, but later on, she came to know about the girl from her co-sister.

The name of the girl was Monalisa, she was from Kolkata and was helpless. She had come to Rourkela to satisfy the lust of the old minister. One day the minister's wife found a pendant under the pillow and had Monalisa's photograph, and there was a fight between the minister and his wife because of this. Since then, the minister's wife didn't sleep on that bed as the minister slept with Monalisa, but he didn't accept his relationship with Monalisa until the end. To give the issue a different perspective, an identity was required for Monalisa. In front of the minister's wife, she was projected as Sanjay Pattnaik's fiancée, and since then, Sanjay Pattnaik has taken care of her. There was an arrangement that was made between Sanjay Pattnaik and Monalisa. Sanjay Pattnaik said that he would convince his parents and get married to her. Sanjay's sister-in-law knew of it, and with a lot of courage, she raised this issue, and the following day, Sanjay was ready with the acquisition that his sister-in-law tried to take advantage of him. After that, her co-sister never discussed Monalisa as she could never muster her courage. Sanjay could convince Monalisa by his words, and she trusted him. Monalisa did whatever she could do so that Sanjay could achieve success in his political career. But one day, while returning from the hospital, Monalisa found... her co-sister didn't complete her words.

After she inquired about it to her co-sister Urbashi, Sanjay Pattnaik said the doctor to perform a hysterectomy on Monalisa so that she would just be a sleeping partner for a man, can never conceive and put the minister and Sanjay in problem. Urbashi was stunned after listening to the conspiracy of Sanjay. She became emotional and held Miki in her arms. She could imagine a devil in Sanjay.

Urbashi raised the topic that night. Sanjay Pattnaik was furious listening to it and pounced on her like an animal. He stripped her clothes and finally declared that she was insane.

Insane!

Urbashi had to live with that identity for four years. She still remembers the torture that she went through. As the Human Rights Commission interfered in her matter, she could come back from Ranchi and try to find out in detail. She wanted to know why and how an ordinary woman like her was branded as insane and how could others accept it?

Urbashi collected a lot of information from Dr. Sibaprasad Mohanty. Dr. Mohanty said that there are two types of insanity. One of them is called Psychosis, and the other one is Neurosis. She was a Psychosis patient, which Dr. Sarangi told. Sanjay had complained, 'Urbashi laughs without any reason and roams around the house half-naked in the presence of her in-laws. She also throws her child, complains about everyone, abuses people at home, and thinks they conspire against her. Sometimes she becomes furious.'

In between, Urbashi had enquired about the symptoms of madness from the doctors. For the past ten years, her life has revolved around the court, hospital, police, and finally, the political leaders. She dreamed that she would teach, write English poetry, do the research work, and go abroad for further studies. She will gain name and fame by becoming an English Professor.

Sanjay Pattnaik proved it in the papers that Urbashi is insane. She was given electroconvulsive therapy, Dialotin and Zapiz tablets were prescribed for her, and finally, as a homeless person, she was sent to Ranchi's mental asylum. Tears dropped from her eyes.

She requested the doctors many times, tried to convince them, and said,' I am not insane. Please send me to my house. If I stay here, then definitely I will become mad.' But the doctors ignored her words as in the certificate and prescription, it was mentioned that she was mentally sick. Doctors can certify that who is insane. Urbashi sometimes wonders, Is there any punishment for the doctors who certify a mentally sound person as insane? She was thrilled when she came to know that the Forest Minister had resigned. She thought it was not enough; the person needed more punishment as he is the creator of injustice. He is a devil in disguise.

Shakuntala knocked at the door and said,' Mr. Pulak has come to give you a packet.'

Urbashi looked uncomfortable as she didn't know anyone named Pulak. Who is this person? Is it the conspiracy of Sanjay Pattnaik?

She couldn't understand whether to say' Yes' or 'No.' Shakuntala left.

Urbashi remembered the thing that happened that

morning. She went to meet the Forest Minister to complain about the way Sanjay tortures and humiliates her. She had faith that he would listen to him as he wasn't only the minister and a well-wisher of her family and the people. If he interferes in this matter, then Sanjay will be able to understand, will behave properly, and life will be normal again. But she was wrong. Urbashi still recalls those two red eyes. As soon as the minister Ramraman saw her, he said,' Why are you spoiling the life of a young man like Sanjay? Let him live peacefully.'

Urbashi didn't expect this from him. Did she spoil the future of Sanjay Pattnaik, or did Sanjay Pattnaik harm her future? Why did Sanjay marry her when he had a kept? Ramraman was chewing the beetle and said,' Urbashi refers to the concubine in the heaven whose work is to satisfy others. Will you be able to satisfy me?'

Urbashi wanted to scream and slap him, but she controlled herself. Why did she come here? This is the Virat city of Mahabharat, where Ramraman himself is the Kichak. She had come here to complain whom against whom? She was scared as she remembered the past. She visited Ramraman's house, which was enough to defame her, and other than that when a husband wants to defame his wife, what's the necessity of others?

'May I come in?'

Urbashi was startled. He is the same young man whom she met in the 'Paduka' shoe store. Why did he come here? She was surprised as the young man sought her permission to enter the room. Someone respected her for the first time in her life as till then; she led a life at the mercy of others. She smiled.

The young man entered the room and gave her a packet. Urbashi asked,' What is this? She also said I met you at the shoe store.'

'You are right. You have met me there, and because of our negligence, you couldn't purchase the sandal and left.'

'Negligence! No ,no' . Urbashi said. She remembered that after meeting Bharat Mahapatra while returning, her sandal broke. She held her sandal in her hand, walked for a distance, and then entered a shoe store to purchase a pair of sandals. She liked the black color sandal which was in the showcase. She ordered her size and waited for some time, and before it could come, she left the place because she didn't have enough money in her purse to purchase the sandal.

'Our salesman Adarsh is a little lazy. Madam, I am sorry for that. Please take the sandal that you liked.'

Urbashi was surprised. Is the young man insane? Maybe it is the first shoe store in Odisha that provides a home delivery facility to the customers. It looked mysterious to her.

The young man opened the packet and kept the sandal near Urbashi's feet. He said,' Wear these sandals from 'Paduka' in your beautiful feet.'

Urbashi laughed. She said,' Do you belong to the secret agency? How did you come to know about my address?'

'How will I not know about your address? Was your photograph not featured in the weekly, and besides that, I got a visiting card from a reporter where you were sitting?' I took your address from him.'

'Maybe I left Bharat Mahapatra's card there. But you traveled from Bhubaneswar to Cuttack and that....

' You are not able to accept it. Isn't it?' The young man said.

'Yes'

'But a customer leaving our store without making any purchase wasn't acceptable for me.'

'But if I say that I didn't have enough money to purchase so I left the store?'

'I will believe you, but our salesman could have been prompt.'

'Is your name Pulak?'

My name is Pulak Mahapatra, and the store belongs to my father, Debendra Mahapatra. I was there at the counter that day. He said all these at a go. Urbashi didn't wear the sandal till then because she was staring at Pulak. Pulak may be a year or two older than her, but Urbashi looked more senior than Pulak.

Urbashi got up from her bed to give him the money. Pulak Mahapatra said, 'If you don't mind, can I request you something?'

'What?' Urbashi sat down.

'Can you accept this as a gift from my side?'

'No,' Urbashi said firmly.

'I knew that a stone-hearted woman like you would give this answer.'

'Stone-hearted? Urbashi was surprised. She said,' After reading a feature about me, how can you guess about my personality?'

'It's not that. You are worried about the payment for a lifeless thing like the sandal, but you didn't ask me for a glass of water on this hot sunny day, and from this, I could guess that you are a stone-hearted person.'

Urbashi was silent. She was attracted to the personality of Pulak. What was there in his personality, she couldn't know, but she was impressed.

Pulak said,' I know a little about you. If you think that in this battle you need someone's help, then think about me. You can pay me the amount. I will leave.'

Urbashi didn't understand what to say. Just a few minutes back, she thought they were her near and dear ones who made her homeless, but Pulak Mahapatra, who is unknown to her, seems to be close to her. He has extended a helping hand and also respects her.

Urbashi said, 'I won't pay you today because I want to meet you again. I need your help.'

It seemed as if Pulak was eagerly waiting to listen to Urbashi.

Urbashi said,' Wait a minute! Let me get a glass of water for you.'

CHAPTER 6

ROURKELA

The resignation of the Forest Minister spread like wildfire in Rourkela. His house, situated in Udit Nagar, was crowded as the party people assembled there. Many workers appreciated the ethical values of the minister, and others criticized the waywardness of his son Rajesh.

Sanjay Pattnaik was with the minister for two days and tried to make him understand, but the minister wasn't ready to understand. He thought that he was pressured to resign, and there was a conspiracy behind it. The Chief Minister could have helped him evade the situation, but he didn't, so he resigned from the MLA position. He had a firm belief that the Chief Minister would help him. When the government filed the vigilance case, the Chief Minister had helped him. He was involved in that case, but here he isn't involved, but the Chief Minister immediately accepted his resignation from both posts.

Sanjay Patnaik was the right hand of the Forest Minister. He advised him and said, 'Let's release Rajesh on bail. I will speak to Raghunath Mishra.'

The Forest Minister screamed as he was helpless and said,' Let that black sheep die. His anger was centered on his son, but Sanjay wasn't taken aback by this. The minister loved his son, and he has brought up and molded Rajesh as his heir. Though the responsibility of the Rourkela election was entrusted to Sanjay- everything was done according to Rajesh's instruction. He was a medium to spend the money and to arrange rallies and meetings. The minister never disclosed this to the party's workers, but Sanjay knew that the minister was shaping his son as his heir.

The death of the Dhaba owner's son Jaswant Singh turned the minister's calculation and planning upside down and raised a question mark in his political career. For twenty-five years, he was the uncrowned king in the political scenario of Rourkela, which shook only because of this incident. He was terrified, as if the earth under his feet caved in.

Sanjay Pattnaik was not that much worried like the minister. There was a reason for it. He wasn't at all nervous; instead, he was happy. Because of this issue, he thought both father and son were thrown out of politics at a go. If the minister had resigned for some other reason, Rajesh might have contested for the position, but now there is no chance for Rajesh to contest in the by-election, and in that case, he is the only contestant. Everyone knows that Sanjay Pattnaik is the political manager of the Forest Minister, so the party workers should propose his name.

Does anyone know about his plans? Sanjay was startled when he was about to call the advocate. Later he relaxed and thought that this happens in politics. The heir should be finalized before the dead body could be cremated; otherwise, everything goes upside down. It happened during Indira Gandhi's death. There are so many examples in the history of India regarding this. In this type of situation, courtesy, etiquette, and emotion don't make any sense. Will he remain as a party worker forever? Wouldn't he become a leader ever? At present, the situation is conducive it has to hit the bull's eye. He should get the party ticket to contest the upcoming election by hook or by crook, but the most important thing is who will propose his name? Sanjay knew very well that he had a lot of enemies in the political party in Rourkela, and their number has increased after Urbashi's case. No decision has been taken regarding the divorce case, so others may not support his candidature in this situation; the support of Ramaraman is required. If the Forest Minister suggests his name, then there won't be any problem. He has to put a lot of effort so that the minister will propose his name. He has served him for many years and won't hesitate to continue serving him. What he needs is power. A powerless leader is like a non-venomous snake whose life is worthless.

Sanjay called the advocate and then came and sat near the minister. He caressed his feet and asked,' sir, are you not feeling well? Shall I inform Dr. Sarangi?'

The minister looked at Sanjay. He thought that the man had been with him for nearly eighteen years. He has carried out all his orders and never retaliated. He also took up the responsibility to accept Monalisa as his wife as it was required then, and of course, he has favored Sanjay for that. He has favored many people by giving them the license of liquor shops and contracts but are those people along with him when he is in need?

Sanjay said,' The opposition party President will arrive in Rourkela on Sunday. He intends to create a fuss over here. If he can keep the issue alive till Vidhan Sabha session, he will benefit from that, but you needn't worry as I have already spoken to the advocate. We have to prove that though Rajesh was there and his friends, he still doesn't have any hand in this murder. After all, he is your political heir. How can he be accused?.'

Ramraman looked happy. He thought it was challenging to find such a devoted person like Sanjay, but it's impossible to give the party ticket to Rajesh according to the present situation. Instead, if Sanjay Pattnaik can contest the election, it will be good for him and strike the target. Firstly, the minister can prove that he doesn't have any greed for power, and secondly, the seat will be under his control, and whenever he wants, he can again contest in the election. But he didn't say that to Sanjay.

Sanjay started pressing his feet. Ramraman said,' Before Sunday, call for a meeting of the party workers. The opposition leader has a vigilance case against him. What will he say about policy and ethics? Our ethics is much better than him. If I hadn't resigned from the MLA post, no one would have dared to say anything. There are many cases against the President of the opposition party other than that for his lustful nature …'

Sanjay said,' Kindly leave that responsibility to me. I will make all the necessary arrangements. You may take rest now. In this situation, we shouldn't lose our temper and should think wisely. Let Rajesh get the bail, then we will think about other things.'

'But will he get the bail? Ramraman asked helplessly.

'Why is so much money paid to advocate Mishra? Sanjay said.

Ramraman looked a little bit relaxed.

Sanjay Pattnaik has got brains. The way he threw away his wife from the house, he was amazed seeing that. During the hearing in the court for divorce, Urbashi Pattnaik wanted to take custody of their daughter, but Sanjay defeated her. He argued, 'Urbashi's father has expired, her mother is split between her two sons and spending a helpless life, and Urbashi is mad so she can't take the responsibility of their daughter. It's not justified to say that as the mother has given birth to the child, she can take care of her properly, and for that, a mother is required to have the capability and has to sacrifice; otherwise, the child's life will be spoilt.

On the other hand, the dispute that he has along with his wife doesn't mean that he doesn't like his child. He wants to do something good for his daughter so that she can prosper in her life and in that case their daughter should stay with him. She will not only get the love and affection of her father but also of her grandparents. The day Urbashi becomes normal at that time he can rethink whether to send his daughter to her.'

Sometimes Ramraman gets scared by the intelligence of Sanjay. He has been a family man for the last forty years, but still, he can't raise his voice in front of his wife. His wife openly says that her husband is a characterless drunkard, but he could never dare to oppose her. Sanjay Pattnaik is like a small kid in front of him, but he could discard his educated wife like a worn-out shoe. He has brains so that he could do this.

He said, 'It's enough. Your hands will pain'. Sanjay Pattnaik, with a lot of zeal, continued pressing his feet and said,' I don't feel good when I look at your face. Nothing as such has happened to think and get shattered. Just wait for four more days. I will make some arrangements. I will convince the boys who were with Rajesh, and one of them will state that the Dhaba boy died as he beat him, and after that, there will be a turning point in the case. Have faith in me.'

Ramraman held Sanjay's hand and said,' It is tough to get a faithful companion like you. Kindly help me out in this situation. I will always be grateful to you.'

Sanjay nodded his head and said,' Please, bless me. That's enough.'

Ramraman said,' Today is Wednesday; after three days, the President of the opposition party will arrive. The Chief Minister has been to Delhi, and we have to do something before he returns.'

'I am preparing a memorandum on behalf of the ruling party in Rourkela. All of us have great trust in you and your ability to guide the party. All of us support you. This was an accident, and you aren't involved in it despite that you have given your resignation and have set an example for others.'

-This will be our unanimous proposal.

'From you side?'- Ramraman stopped Sanjay.

' You obeyed the Chief Minister and have taken the initiative to resign from both the posts, and that's a great thing.'

Ramraman wanted to say something and saw Raghunath Mishra entering the room along with his driver.

Advocate Raghunath Mishra straightforwardly said,' sir, the case is complicated.'

Sanjay said, 'If the case had not been difficult, then why would sir have called for an advocate like you? Is there any other advocate who is more capable than you? If so, then let us know so that sir can take his refuge.'

'But the minister's son..'

'Not minister, the Ex-minister.' Ramraman corrected him. When he said 'Ex' the pain on the minister's face was clearly evident.

Advocate Raghunath Mishra could understand. He said,' For us, you are always the minister. This is just like the dark passing clouds, which will slowly go away. It's not necessary to worry much about it. Sir, I was saying, In this case....

'Rajesh babu hasn't killed anyone. The boy who killed has already confessed. 'Sanjay said coolly.

'Is it so? I didn't know that.'

'I will try my best.' Raghunath Mishra said.

Sanjay went into the house to make arrangements for the advocate. After their son was arrested, the minister's wife had confined herself to her room, and now Sanjay had to take all the responsibilities. This is required for his prospects.

Advocate Mishra wanted to discuss a few things with Ramraman alone. After Sanjay left he went and sat near Ramraman.

CHAPTER-7

CUTTACK

It was almost more than one and a half months after Urbashi returned from the opposition party's office, and at that time, she couldn't meet the party President. She neither received any call nor any information from Bharat Mahapatra. Urbashi never believed that Bharat Mahapatra would ever take the initiative and call her on his own. Still, she had a little ray of hope that Bharat may inform the President of the opposition party about her before he left for the opposition party meeting at Rourkela. In between, she tried many times to contact Bharat Mahapatra but failed to do so.

Urbashi thought, 'For how many more days she will stay in 'Ashraya'?' Sometimes she lost her patience and willpower.

'Ashraya' Working Women's Hostel, situated in the Cantonment road, has become her house. But she doesn't have a regular job. If she hadn't left the lecturer's position, that would have helped her to survive. It is painful and disgraceful to stay with the money that she gets from Sanjay Pattnaik, who has discarded her like a rotten object.

Sanjay Pattnaik doesn't want to give the money. He argued that he doesn't have a constant source of income and he is surviving on his father's money. His father didn't get any property as an heir, so according to the law, the son and daughter-in-law can't demand anything from the property. Other than that, he has the responsibility of a mentally ill son. Their daughter Miki is also staying with him, so it's not easy to give any amount to Urbashi every month with so much responsibility.

Urbashi's situation was like a person in the middle of the ocean. Water! Water! Everywhere but not a drop to drink. Her parents have a lot of property, so are her in-laws, but no one has the money to give her.

Sanjay Pattnaik doesn't want that she should survive, so why will he give her money? Her brothers and sister-in-laws thought that they had already done their duty by getting her married. It's a wastage to spend money for a married girl. The matter would have been different if the situation had been good. If they had gotten any help and respect from Urbashi's in-law's house, then they could have tried to be in touch with her. But they thought it was not necessary to keep any relationship with the dishonored sister's family. Urbashi feels uncomfortable when she remembers these. She could very well realize the ingenuous countenance of her near and dear ones under the mask. She sometimes feels like dragging them to the court to get her rights. Suppose she could tell them that what they wish or not isn't the law of this country, and according to the law, a married daughter has equal rights over paternal property. But she feels helpless without any support. If she has to file a case against anyone, she has to go to the advocate, and for that, she requires money, and there is also a court fee. Even if she signs the vakalatnama, then no one will fight her case. The more she was thinking about it, the more helpless she was. She would have never lost the case against Ramraman. Still, she was betrayed by a voluntary organization, 'Sahajog' in Rourkela, which claimed itself as an organization that helps women to get their rights.

Urbashi approached Ms. Nalini of 'Sahajog' for help. Urbashi told her everything in detail. She told Ms. Nalini about Ramraman and Sanjay's relationship, Monalisa Dutta's hysterectomy, and Ramraman's bad behaviour towards her. Ms. Nalini convinced her to rely on her, keep quiet, not tell anyone about it, and have patience. Urbashi kept her face on Ms. Nalin's lap and cried a lot. Ms. Nalini consoled her and said that this bad time would be over soon and there was nothing to worry about. She said,' You may come and stay here. We will fight your case. There are still good people in the world. Justice still prevails, there is Women Commission, and still, there are courts in Odisha.'

Urbashi stayed in 'Sahajog' for a month and waited for a counteraction, but Ms. Nalini never made any effort to proceed further. She lost her patience. She was surprised that a woman like Ms. Nalini, who retaliates against injustice, is quiet. She realized that Ms. Nalini was trying to utilize her as a pawn in the politics of the voluntary organization. The building of 'Sahajog' was constructed on land worth twenty-five lakhs. Ms. Nalini requested the government to give that land on lease to them, but Mr. Ramraman opposed it. Ms. Nalini, who belonged to the Leftist organization, wasn't on good terms with Rammaran, but Urbashi and Monalisa's episode was enough to get Ramraman in trouble. By the time Urbashi came to know about it, Ramraman had already made arrangements to give the land on lease to the organization. Not only that, he purchased a house in Kolkata for Monalisa and settled her through women leader Ms. Nalini.

She was surprised when she looked at Ms. Nalini that day. She never thought that a woman who wears a simple saree doesn't wear any ornaments and is an insurgent has such an ugly reality. Ms. Nalini was greedy for power and money, which Urbashi never imagined.

Urbashi remembered the story of 'The swan in Mansarovar and the disguised sage'. She read the story some time back.

A king of a kingdom fell sick. No one could cure him, so the royal doctor advised, if the swan in the Mansarovar is brought alive, burnt, and fed to the king, he will get well soon. After a lot of effort, they realized that catching the swan in Mansarovar wasn't easy. The king's health was deteriorating day by day. In the meantime, a gentleman came and assured that he would bring the swan of Mansarovar alive. All of them were surprised to listen to him, but the gentleman ignored their apprehension. He took a hundred thousand gold coins from the kingdom's treasury and left to get the swan. The minister and the chieftain thought that the cunning and greedy man had left and would never return again. Still, the queen didn't comment on anything because the gentleman was supposed to get another hundred thousand gold coins as a prize after getting the swan. After five days, the gentleman came to the king's court. He brought along with him two swans from Mansarovar. All of them were surprised. They couldn't understand how an ordinary man could do what the chieftain and his soldiers couldn't do?

After receiving the prize money, the gentleman said,'

Maharani! The swans of Mansarovar crave knowledge and love the presence of saints. When the chieftain went along with his soldiers on the horse, the swans were scared and swam away. Maybe it was possible to kill them though they were far and bring their bodies, but it wasn't possible to bring them alive. I went along with four other companions, and we collected the dresses and other necessary props that a saint uses from a shop selling the costumes for dance and drama. We wore those costumes and looked like saints. Then we reached the bank of Mansarovar and chanted the shlokas which we have by-hearted. When the swans of Mansarovar heard us chanting the shlokas, they swam and came near us. When they were within our reach, we pretended as if we were trying to caress them and caught hold of their neck, and then kept them in our bag and brought them here. We could have got many more, but the king requires only one.'

Ms. Nalin's behavior wasn't different from the behaviour of the saints in disguise. Ms. Nalini knowingly made her case weak, and Ramraman could easily escape. After that, she had no other way other than leaving 'Sahajog'. She thought it was better to die than to live and take the favor of such a woman. A woman who exploits the opportunity arising out of the condition of another woman and a broker is more dangerous than a person like Ramraman. She did not doubt it.

Sometimes Urbashi thinks about Monalisa. Where will the girl be? Monalisa's fate was worse than her fate, a victim of Ramraman and Sanjay who talks about helping the needy. At least Urbashi has a daughter though she doesn't stay with her. She is still living a normal life of a woman, but Monalisa doesn't have that. She is just leading her life like a machine.

Her co-sister had told her that Monalisa was a greedy woman. Money and jewelry is the prime thing in her life; that's why it isn't necessary to feel pity for her. But even a concubine also has the right to live. Urbashi said- Why can't Monalisa have the right to decide about her life? She should know why did they perform a hysterectomy? But Monalisa never protested. Was she happy and content with the past misfortune and the prosperity of the future, or did she not dare to oppose? Urbashi couldn't answer that.

Urbashi came to the balcony and looked at the sky. It was almost four days after Dussehra and the next day was Kumar Purnima. The early morning of autumn was filled with the soft rays of the sun. The tiny droplets of water on the grass were shining like the gemstones in the sunray. On one corner of the garden, there was a barren Crepe jasmine tree. Was it affected by insects because just a few months back, flowers bloomed on the tree? Now it's barren; there isn't a single leaf on the tree. All the leaves from the tree had fallen one by one. This Crepe jasmine tree now looks like a girl whose hair has been tonsured. But she was amazed by a scene of a dying Crepe jasmine tree but a butterfly sitting on the barren tree though there were many plants in the garden which had flowers and leaves.

It's astonishing- Urabashi spoke to herself, and at that time, she remembered Pulak. Pulak is constantly in touch with her from the day he brought the sandals for her. In between, he had come twice to meet her. He was there along with Urbashi for a long time and both of them went together to Gadagadia ghat to roam around. In one of the songs of Akshaya Mohanty, it is mentioned about Gadagadiya ghat where the young girls and boys go to eat Dahi bara and Alu Dum. Pulak gave a lot of hope to Urbashi. Now she remembered about what Pulak said, looking at the barren Crepe jasmine tree.

Pulak came to Urbashi's life too late. Urbashi thought about it and jerked. It's a sin, her conservative mind warned her. She is the wife of someone, and it doesn't matter if he is trying his best to give him a divorce. She is Miki's mother; that's why it's a sin to think about any other man.

Miki! She is her daughter. She is the representation of her flesh and blood, her thoughts and soul. She hasn't seen her for a long time. Last year Sanjay Pattnaik had brought her to the court only once. By that time, they had already proved that Urbashi was insane. Her eleven years old daughter Miki couldn't recognize her mother, but Urbashi could recognize her immediately. She is her daughter. She has spent one and half years with her telling her stories and singing lullaby for her. She tried to forget the torture that she underwent looking at the baby. Sanjay Pattnaik doesn't allow her to see Miki. He justifies it by saying,' Her mother is mad. She is a witch. She will kill his daughter.'

The judge asked Miki with whom will she stay? Miki replied that she has rotely learned,' If I go to my mad mother, she will kill me. I will stay with my father and my grandparents.'

Urbashi's motherhood was mocked in the court, but she didn't feel bad. It doesn't matter where Miki stays; after all, she is her daughter. She would have never preferred Miki to be divided between the parents. If she had done that, then where would she have kept Miki? How would she have taken care of her? How would she have fed her? Let her be with that demon but let her live happily.'

Urbashi was crying. She was longing to see Miki. She wiped her tears, and at that time, someone knocked at the door. She got irritated and shouted,' Who is that?'

Pulak said,' Kindly excuse me. Maybe I came at the wrong time. He was holding a withered grass flower. Urbashi felt a little uncomfortable. She was feeling guilty because of her rude behavior. Pulak is the only person who has been helping her for the past one and half months. What would he have thought?

'Pulak, I thought there was someone else at the door.'

As the prince offered the rose to his kinswoman similarly, Pulak gave the withered grass flower to Urbashi. Urbashi couldn't understand whether to laugh or cry. She said, 'Yesterday I was remembering you.'

'Does anyone remember a joker?'

'Who is a joker?'

Pulak said,' Mera name Joker' and sat on the table. He gave Urbashi the English newspaper.

Urbashi said, 'Is there anything about me again?'

'No, no I wanted to show you something else.' Pulak said and then opened the newspaper and showed her an article. The heading of the article was' This was the most beautiful flower.' Urbashi read the article.

One day for some reason, a woman was upset. She went and sat in the corner of a park. At that time a boy came to her. He showed him the grass flower and said,' Look, isn't it a beautiful flower?' The woman who was already irritated got more irritated. She wanted to shout at the boy and look at his face, and suddenly her anger vanished like the water bubbles as the boy was blind.

How can a blind person see that a sad woman was sitting in the corner of the park and change her mood? Does he need a flower? After that, she accepted the flower from the boy happily. She was excited and said,' Yes, this is the most beautiful flower in the world.' The blind boy happily ran into the park and collected another grass flower, and ran in the other direction, maybe searching for another sad person.

The woman was impressed by the perceiving power of the blind boy. As the dark clouds similarly subside from the sky, her anger subsided. Urbashi now understood the meaning of Pulak bringing the grass flower. Pulak is thinking about her so profoundly, but why? Who is she for Pulak? What is her relationship with Pulak? They met accidentally as two passengers in a train meet while traveling, and as they reach their destination, they go in their way. What will be left behind are the memories of the time that they have spent in the train compartment.

Pulak said,' The other day, you were talking about suicide. What is suicide? It is an ugly allegation about our identity. Did any philosopher ever say anything about it?'

'But I am not able to tolerate it anymore Pulak. I am not able to.'

'Look at this grass flower and think about the story of the blind boy. You have to be firm. I will be there with you till you need me, and the day you say that you don't need me that day, I will go away from your life as I came to your life.'

'But how will this benefit you? Why are you wasting your precious time for me?'

'It isn't a wastage of time without any reason. In this world, all human beings aren't selfish. Is it a wastage of time to build someone's confidence?'

'You should have read Philosophy instead of Literature.' Urbashi said. She took the grass flower in hand and kept it carefully.

Pulak said,' I will go to Delhi for a week, and I have come to inform you about it. I will again meet you after I return.'

Urbashi suddenly had the feeling of loneliness. Pulak visits him sometimes, but why did she feel lonely today when she heard that Pulak would be going to Delhi for a week? This feeling is different from the feeling that you get when you lose something precious. Why is it a different feeling?

She said, 'If you knew that you would be in this shoe business, then why did you go to Delhi for further studies?'

'Just to become a learned businessman, nothing else.'

'This isn't an answer to my question.' Urbashi said.

Pulak smiled. He stood up and looked outside.' My father qualified for the Civil Services of India but didn't pursue his job, but I thought I would do a job. But …

'What is that 'But'? You have an outstanding academic career; you could have taken up a good job.'

'I was studying at Delhi University almost thirteen to fourteen years back. Few incidents happened which led me to decide to change my decision.' Pulak stopped for a while and said,' Our business is doing well. What I would have gained more by taking up a job?'

Urbashi could understand that Pulak was trying to hide something. She didn't force him to say. Who knows Pulak also might be having some sorrows in life. Who doesn't have problems in this world? She said, 'Pulak; I am unable to tolerate it anymore. I am tired. All of them say that one should help the weak, they write in the newspaper and magazine, but they don't support when required. Can I do anything alone?'

Pulak remained quiet for some time and then said,' I believe that there is always a solution to whenever there is a problem. You might have noticed that when a disease spreads in an area, the medicine or the treatment is available nearby.'

Urbashi was startled. Does she have a solution to the problem?

Suddenly there was a glow on her face. She became enthusiastic, and her enthusiasm couldn't evade Pulak's eyes. He asked, 'What are you thinking?'

'The problem comes with a solution.'

'Oh! I thought that you got an idea to solve the problem.'

Urbashi said,' After listening to you, I have an idea, but I need your help in this regard. Will you help me?'

Pulak was silent, but he was smiling. Urbashi said,' Can you call the reporter Bharat Mahapatra and tell him something?'

'About what?'

Urbashi told him what she meant. Pulak nodded his head and gave a proposal. Urbashi was stunned when she heard his proposal, but Pulak assured her, and there was a sense of relief reflected on her face.

Urbashi said,' Pulak, can I ask you something?'

'You may ask.'

'Don't others take you in a wrong way because you come to meet me?'

'Are you feeling bad?' Pulak asked in return.

'I am branded as characterless. What can be worse than this?'

Pulak said,' I don't require any certificate.'

Urbashi was shy, as if she asked him an absurd question. Pulak looked at Urbashi's face and said,' Can I ask you a question?'

Urbashi was silent, which meant that Pulak shouldn't be too formal.

'Why are you so callous about your life? Look at the mirror and check how you look defeated. If you lose the war before it begins, then the opponent will be motivated. Take care of yourself. At least don't look as if you are defeated, and always remember that you aren't the only woman in this world who is sad. No one in this world is alone, not even a blind person, a physically disabled person, a happy or sad person. People with the same fate who live in this world may be in different places. There may be many women like you in thousands who are suffering like you or more than you. The difference between them and you is that they have accepted that as their fate, whereas you think it is an atrocity and oppose it. You want to stand against injustice. But if a person who wants to fight against injustice becomes mentally weak, how will others trust her? Why will they come forward to help her? '

Urbashi could understand what Pulak wanted to convey, but she was silent. Pulak was about to leave.

Urbashi never goes behind Pulak when he leaves, but that day she couldn't stop herself. Lisa and Shymala, those who were staying in the next room, were looking at her. Urbashi didn't feel bad about it, and she followed Pulak confidently.

Pulak went away. Urbashi stood near the gate for a long time and looked in that direction.

CHAPTER- 8

CAPITAL

'Bloody Fool! Irresponsible!' The President of the opposition party shouted. The news published on the first page of 'OSF India' made him worried. He pressed the buzzer of the telephone, and Mr. Sarangi lifted the phone. He said,' Call the reporter Bharat Mahapatra immediately and tell him to meet me.'

There was a reason for his annoyance. The reporter of the newspaper 'OSF India' wrote that the President of the opposition party has decided to give the ticket to a lady to contest Rourkela's by-election. In the past, this lady was tortured by her husband, and she complained that the Forest Minister also misbehaved with her. According to the President of the opposition party, the lady will play the role of Draupadi like in Mahabharata to wipe out the Jungle Raj of the Forest Minister. Bharat Mahapatra also wrote that the President of the opposition party had a preliminary discussion about it.

The President was thinking about the irresponsible behavior of Bharat Mahapatra and the audacity of the lady. He had never met the lady though she had come to the party office once and had tried to meet him. She might have come to the party office, but he doesn't have any information regarding it. Every day many people come to meet him, and he can't satisfy everyone. Maybe the lady has given this information to Bharat Mahapatra. But how can Bharat Mahapatra do such careless reporting? Is the man mad, or has the lady influenced him? Whatever it is, but today the explanation has to be published. He hasn't yet decided anything regarding Rourkela, and if he takes any decision without the knowledge of the Political Trade Committee, then Harekrusha and Ashok will create havoc.

The phone rang, and Mr. Sarangi informed him that Bharat Mahapatra wasn't there in his house. The President became restless. At present, he needed someone who could do the work immediately. He said,' Send the vehicle to fetch him as it's urgent.'

When the President of the opposition party was searching for Bharat Mahapatra, he was sitting quietly in his house. The situation was such that he couldn't step out of his house. Right from the morning, the other reporters were continuously calling him. He has never made such a blunder in his reporting career, and that's why he was in the house still; he wasn't answering the calls. Other than to hide and to remain quiet for some time, he had no other options.

Yesterday, someone from the opposition party's office called him, telling him that he is Mr. Surendra, his spokesperson. He knows Mr. Surendra very well, so there was no reason not to believe in what he said. After he received the information, he called 'Ashraya' in Cuttack. After calling four to five times, finally around ten-thirty in the evening, he could speak to Ms. Urbashi Pattnaik. Urbashi Pattnaik informed him that just an hour back, she had received this information from the party office, and after that, there was no reason from the reporter Bharat Mahapatra to have any doubt. He thought that he should publish this news in the newspaper before others could, so he gave the information to his newspaper editor. There is tough competition among the reporters regarding any statement. Though they behave friendly with each other, they don't share the information that they have. In this way, there is always an invisible competition between them day in and out, and in the morning, it comes to light which has won the match. Whoever is late in collecting the information is the loser. Bharat Mahapatra thought that he would give this fresh news and win the race. But he realized in the morning that it was fake news.

The lady is shrewd- Bharat Mahapatra thought and planned for the next step. He is very much scared of the President of the opposition party. He has got a bungalow in the capital because of him, and the rest envy him for this- other than that, he has also got a car. If the gentleman gets annoyed and takes any steps against him, it will be difficult for him, so it will be better to meet him and tell him the actual story. The opposition party President is in politics for a long time to trust him, but what will he say to the Editor? He is constantly annoyed and compares him with the reporter Amiya Kar of 'New Odiya Express'. According to him, Amiya Kar is objective, analytical, and daredevil, and Bharat Mahapatra is only a Press Release reporter. Bharat could genuinely feel what problem this piece of news was going to create for him. He was feeling helpless thinking about it. Instead of going to Bhubaneswar Club, he should have called Mr. Surendra to confirm the matter again. Then, he could have evaded the trouble, but the time had slipped out of his hand.

He went to the opposition party President's house 'Taruna Tirtha'. It was twenty minutes drive from his house, but for these twenty minutes, he was anxious.

Mr. Sarangi saw him and was happy. He said,' I have sent the vehicle to fetch you. Where were you? Sir is looking for you.'

'Is there anyone inside?'

'Who else will be there other than Urbashi Pattnaik. She is here right from the morning. Sir will hand her over to the police.'

'Shall I go?'

-' Wait, let me take the permission; otherwise, I will get the scolding. I can't do this job anymore, Bharat babu. Who will work with this short-tempered old man?'

Mr. Sarangi pushed the telephone extension buzzer. When he pressed the buzzer, he looked normal, but the expression on his face changed after keeping the receiver down.

'What did he say?' Bharat Mahapatra asked.

'Idiot !' Mr. Sarangi said

'That means am I an idiot?- Bharat Mahapatra couldn't tolerate this in the presence of two other people.

'Not you; it's me.' Sir told me not to disturb him now.

'Thank God!' Now you can order coffee. I am unable to think anything right from the morning.'

'You can have four cups instead of one cup, but don't leave this place; otherwise, I will lose my job. You are all horrible people. You make small things a big issue and print those in your newspaper.

Bharat Mahapatra didn't give any reply to what Mr. Sarangi said and looked around. Mr. Sarangi understood that Bharat Mahapatra doesn't want to discuss the issue in front of others. He told other people who were present there to go.

Two of them who were sitting there understood the indication and left. Now he was sitting alone with Mr. Sarangi in that bungalow.

Bharat Mahapatra said,' Yesterday, Mr. Surendra informed me regarding this over the phone.'

'No, Mr. Surendra has been there in Paralakhemundi for the last two days. Maybe someone else called you and told his name falsely. Some people even duplicate the party letterhead and send a fax to the newspaper. You are so much experienced, but why didn't you cross-check?'

'That is the mistake I did, and for that, I am in trouble otherwise, did anyone dare to point fingers at Bharat Mahapatra till now? Ok, tell me, who is the candidate from your party for Rourkela's by-election?'

'Nothing has been decided yet. Many people in the queue have expectations. Let the old man select.'

'I made a great mistake.'

'Sir is very much annoyed. You remain quiet. He has high blood pressure. If you say something, we will be in trouble as sir has to go to Delhi today.'

Bharat sat quietly. The peon brought coffee and served it.

Mr. Sarangi asked the peon,' Did that lady come out of the room?

The peon said, 'No.'

'Today, the lady will learn a lesson. She will never dare to come here again.' Mr. Sarangi laughed wickedly.

Bharat didn't say anything. He wasn't in a good mood. He was looking at his watch. It was almost an hour, but still, the discussion was going on. What is he discussing with Urbashi Pattnaik for such a long time?

He said, 'Mr. Sarangi, can you please go and check? I have not yet taken a bath.'

Mr. Sarangi said,' No, who will go to the tiger's den now? Just wait. I think within half an hour, the discussion will be over. Sir will get ready to go to Delhi.'

'What is Urbashi Pattnaik discussing?'

'How do I know? Rather you should know about it as you took her to the party office for the first time. She might be narrating her sad story, or the old man might be scolding her, and she might be crying. If once the old man starts scolding, then it continues for hours. Did you understand?'

Bharat wasn't thinking about Urbashi Pattnaik; rather, he was thinking about himself. After that, he has to call the Editor and listen to his scolding. By this time, others would have already informed him. Sandeep Ray, who is expecting to be the candidate from Rourkela, must have already called the Editor. Last time he was defeated by Ramraman in a few votes, so his chance of winning the election is more this time. He must be thinking that Bharat Mahapatra and the party workers who are against him have tried to uproot him. Politics is amazing! Here the leaders of the same party are against each other in the party. Sandeep Ray sits with the MLAs of other parties in the hotel and has drinks with them, but he never speaks to Harekrushna, Prasanth, or Ajay, who belong to his party. Of course, this isn't only the culture of the opposition party but also the culture of the ruling party. The relationship between Rajsekhar Mohanty and Sadanand Biswal is also not good. Suppose the defection rule wouldn't have been so rigid. In that case, he might have already taken ten to fifteen MLAs into confidence and would have brought the ruling government down, but to bring the government down, the support of a minimum of twenty-seven MLAs is required.

Mr. Sarangi's telephone buzzer rang. He received the phone. He spoke over the phone and said to Bharat Mahapatra,' You may go into the room.'

Bharat Mahapatra arranged his hair and walked towards the room of the President. He was tensed.

As soon as the President saw Bharat Mahapatra, he screamed, 'Come in, the irresponsible reporter.'

Bharat Mahapatra didn't like how the party President addressed him as an irresponsible reporter in front of someone else. He didn't appreciate it but tolerated it. He smiled and greeted him and saw Urbashi sitting in front of the party President. Urbashi looked at him, smiled, and greeted him. She said softly, 'Pardon me, Mr. Bharat.'

Bharat Mahapatra didn't tell her anything. He didn't reflect his annoyance on the face, but he softly said Urbashi,' I will speak to you when you go outside. Did you not find anyone else to betray?' He said to the party President,' I will publish your defense note today. It was a misunderstanding....'

Are you sure that your Editor will tolerate it? He called me in the morning. Bharat Mahapatra was startled and looked helpless. It would have been better if he had called the Editor and would have spoken to him. At least he would have got some more time to understand the matter, but he didn't do that and is now facing the consequences. The party President said firmly,' Bharat Mahapatra, you are an irresponsible reporter.' He was shattered thinking about the results.

The party President said,' You take an interview of Urbashi because you have only two options in front of you. One option is to publish a note on the mistake you have made, and the other option is to prove the mistake as truth.'

'Sir, I couldn't understand.'

'We are thinking of giving her the ticket as a candidate from our party for Rourkela's by-election.' The party President said this as if he was announcing an important decision.

'Means?' Bharat Mahapatra was surprised. He went along with Urbashi Pattnaik to meet the party President, but it was just casually; otherwise, he didn't sympathize with her. After that- the incident that happened yesterday. From that incident, he can infer that Urbashi is very intelligent. He gave his views to the party President on his decision and said,' Madam is a dangerous lady.'

The party President interrupted him in between and said,' I think you know that I like dangerous ladies.'

Bharat Mahapatra was stunned. Of course, the party President's decision will bring some relief to him as his wrong information was going to be proved as correct. Others will publish the news today. But by that time, he would have already taken the interview of Urbashi Pattnaik and published the follow-up report, and he will be ahead of others in collecting the information. Despite that, he can never pardon Urbashi Pattnaik. He brought Urbashi to meet the party President, but she couldn't meet him, so now he should be happy for Urbashi's achievement, but he wasn't happy at all. Till yesterday Urbashi was after him, and now Urbashi has superseded him without any help or cooperation. His psyche couldn't accept this.

He said to the party President,' There is a saying in English, 'I don't know the key to success, but the key to failure is trying to please everybody.' Soon the boss will call the PSC, and a decision will be taken regarding this matter.'

Bharat Mahapatra is a dexterous reporter. He knew that the decision of the party President was the ultimate decision. He tried his best to stop Urbashi from taking this chance and said,' sir, the woman who has betrayed her family members, how do you expect that she will be loyal to the party?'

Urbashi contradicted this statement. The party President indicated her to keep quiet and said,' In this world, there are many sons who have killed their fathers either to get the property or for the throne, but there isn't a single daughter who has killed her father for the power. Can you give any example?'

'But what about Sandeep Ray?'

'The Political Affairs Committee will decide about it. You may leave now.'

Bharat understood that the party President didn't want to discuss with him regarding the party matter. He stood up. The party President said mockingly,' Don't ever forget that I did all this to save your job.'

Bharat wasn't happy. This is said 'Killing with kindness.' He left the room.

After Bharat Mahapatra left the room, the party President said to Urbashi,' My vehicle will drop you in Cuttack. You will immediately pack your luggage and leave that place. You will go with me to Delhi. We will discuss other things later on.'

Urbashi asked, 'What about my ticket to Delhi?'

He said,' Mr. Sarangi must have already booked the flight ticket.'

Urbashi looked at her wristwatch. It was almost 11 O'Clock. She has to go to Cuttack and return. She has never taken a flight before. This will be her first experience.

While going back to Cuttack, she was thinking about her discussion with the party President. She couldn't understand how she could gather so much courage? She could only remember that the things in her heart had narrated everything to the party President for such a long time. He knew that she was telling the truth, and there was not a bit of a lie in what she spoke. She cried and told him her pain, helplessness, and about her humiliation.

When she came to meet the party president, she was terrified. She knew that he is a very short-tempered person. Sometimes he raises his hand to hit others, but as she was a lady, he may not do that but may humiliate her. If he does, then that will break her heart. She thought that when she met the party President at that time, other party workers would be present, and he would scold her in front of them, but there is a lot of difference between apprehension and reality. She couldn't trust her experience with him.

She was remembering Pulak. The man is brilliant, and she never thought that his plan would work.

CHAPTER-9

CAPITAL

In the opposition party office at Forest Park, the Political Trade Committee meeting was called. The by-election was in the first week of January. The ruling party had announced Sanjay Pattnaik, the youth party leader, as their candidate for the by-election. His name was proposed by the Ex- Forest minister Ramraman and the high command approved it out of sympathy. There is a difference in opinion between Chief Minister Rajsekhar Mohanty and Sports Minister Sadanand Biswal, like the difference in view which was seen in the sixties between Radhakrushna Chowdhary and Mahaparata Mahadev, so it won't be difficult for the opposition party to win if Sandeep Ray becomes the opposition party candidate.

Urbashi Pattnaik is limiting his chance. After returning from Delhi, the opposition party President is firm in his decision that other than Urbashi Pattnaik, he will not accept anyone else as the candidate. All of them are aware of the party President's impatient nature and irritating behavior; that's why no one dares to oppose him, but they weren't happy from within.

The main reason to oppose Urbashi Pattnaik's candidature was Sandeep Ray was an industrialist, and he donates to the party fund. Many party workers were loyal to him for this.

The party President asked,' Harekrushna tell me what to do?'

Harekrushna looked at the other party workers and said clearly,' We have to think about Sandeep Ray. He is disciplined and an old member of our party.'

'He will go to the Rajya Sabha,' The party President said. All of them, including Harekrushna Pattnaik, were surprised listening to this. In April, there will be three vacant positions in Rajya Sabha. According to the present situation, despite the conspiracy of Rajsekhar, the opposition party will win at least one seat. There are many expecting candidates in the party, but the President didn't announce Sandeep Ray.

Ashok Samal said,' How is it justified to make an insane person the candidate for the by-election?'

The party President looked at Ashok Samal and said,' Tell me how many insane people have you seen? I have seen gentlemen throwing the garbage of their house on the road, but a mad man picks up that garbage, rags, and cleans the road.'

'Sir, I couldn't understand.' Ashok Samal said.

'Urbashi was along with me for three days. I have observed her for three days. She has all the qualities to be the leader of the mass. She has the passion, zeal, enthusiasm, and the will to do something new. We couldn't have got a better candidate than Urbashi against Sanjay Pattnaik. If you listen to her good thoughts, then all of you will be impressed by that. I can say confidently that she isn't mad. It was a conspiracy. Other than that, have you ever thought about why a person becomes insane? Those who dupe others are considered appropriate people in society. Those duped by others on the family front, in love, business, or politics are branded as insane. The result of the by-election will be valid for only two and a half years. Whoever wins will be the MLA for two and half years. If we lose the seat, then the Chief Minister Rajsekhar Mohanty will get encouraged, but if Urbashi wins, then have you ever thought how much laurel it will bring to our party?' The President asked.

Sanjay Mohanty asked,' If the new people will come and take the ticket every time, how will the party benefit? How will the old members and the leaders in the party have the zeal to work?'

The party President smiled and said,' The same question was asked me by Harekrushna when you were a candidate. At that time, you were a newcomer to this party. Today both of you are present here so that you may ask Harekrushna. He can answer your question.'

There was a difference in opinion in the meeting. The party President knew that his followers couldn't understand. He is an old player in Odisha's politics. He is like a player in the center forward on a football ground and has been in this for forty-five years. Many have come and have left, but he is still in that position.

The party President said,' I have knowingly taken Urbashi to Delhi along with me. If she had been here, then people would have asked her many things. Maybe she couldn't have handled the press reporters properly. In these three days, I have come to know a lot about her. I am confident that we will win that seat.'

The party President said the things very clearly, so

there was no chance for others to retaliate. If they argue more than Sandeep Ray's candidature for Rajya Sabha will be doubtful. It's also a good deal for Sandeep Ray as the tenure in Vidhan Sabha will be for only two and half years, but as a candidate in Lok Sabha, he will have a term for six years. If the situation at that time is conducive, then he may become a minister in the center.

Harikrishna said,' After the meeting, kindly inform Sandeep to discuss with me. I want that he should go to Rourkela and propose Urbashi's candidature. '

Ashok said,' Sandeep isn't there in the capital.'

'Who said that he isn't there? Yesterday he returned from Rourkela.' The party President said. They looked at each other's faces as no one knew about it, but the party President had the information. Is he omnipresent? The party President is keeping an eye on Sandeep Ray. In the year 1971, there was turmoil in Odisha's political scenario. Two newly-elected MLAs left 'Taruna Tirtha' and hid in the house of an MLA of the ruling party. At that time, the party President went in his station wagon and brought those two MLAs forcefully. If the party President knows that Sandeep Ray has returned from Rourkela, he must know. It's better to listen to what he is saying rather than argue with him. It will be beneficial for the party as well for Sandeep Ray.

Political Trade Committee accepted the party President's proposal. Urbashi Pattnaik will be the contestant from the opposition party, and the party will try its best to win. The downfall of the Chief Minister's party in Rourkela will be the aim of the opposition party.

When in the opposition party's office, the proposal of

Urbashi Pattnaik was accepted at that time in Ramraman's government quarters, the ruling party was discussing their final strategy. In between, Rajesh got the bail, so Ramraman was a little relaxed. He was exploring and making strategies about how Sanjay Pattnaik will win the election. He knew that Sanjay Pattanik was very faithful to him and supported him. If he wins the seat from Rourkela, then it will be like his victory. If Sanjay Pattnaik loses the election, that will end his political career so he won't be affected by anything. He has the proof of Sanjay's misdeed, so if at any point in time Sanjay wants to surpass him, then with the help of those proves, he can again bring him to track.

Sanjay has taken a vow in Panposh's Tarini temple that he will be following all the instructions of Ramraman. He will be a representative of him from the Rourkela seat. Till Ramraman is alive, he is the only leader of Rourkela, and no one should dare to look at that seat. Even if Sanjay Pattnaik wins the seat in the by-election and becomes the MLA, he will still leave his seat during the election to Ramraman. This arrangement was the political strategy to handle the present situation.

His vow had impressed the workers of the ruling party in Rourkela. At Bhubaneswar, the state-level leaders were impressed by the loyalty of Sanjay. In between, the youth leader Bimalendu Mahapatra had acquired a lot of information about Sanjay Pattnaik. He asked, 'Will the decision of the opposition party to propose Urbashi Pattnaik as the candidate will land us in trouble?'

Sanjay Pattnaik answered immediately. He said,' Rather they have made it easy for us. I regret that once she was my wife.'

Bimalendu interrupted and said,' What do you mean by once? Till now, the judgment hasn't come for your divorce case.'

A decision will be taken in between regarding the case. Other than that, everyone in Rourkela knows that she is insane. Her father and brothers didn't ask about her well-being. Whoever gave her shelter, she went against them. She wanted to bring disgrace to Ramraman sir, who is of her father's age. She didn't even spare the renowned volunteer of Rourkela, Ms. Nalini; other than that; she created a lot of trouble in the family. The opposition party can only select a candidate like her who is a nasty lady.

Others laughed loudly. This is the image of the opposition leader about the women. Previously, he had allowed many beautiful women and placed them in the corporation and municipality in a high position. That had become a state-level discussion. Sanjay Pattnaik took advantage of the opportunity and didn't refrain from giving such comments about his wife and made fun of her with other party members. After the lighter moments, he folded his hands and sought everyone's cooperation. As there was only a month left, he requested all the experienced leaders of the party to go to Rourkela for campaigning.

Ramraman said,' I will look after those things. You may go back to Rourkela tomorrow and make arrangements to open the office. Call for party workers meeting on Sunday. On that day, the booth committee will be formed, and the responsibilities will be allotted.'

'What about the Chief Minister's program?' Sanjay asked.

Bimal Mahapatra, the youth leader, had a good rapport with the ruling party leader Rajsekhar Mohanty. Ramraman looked at him. Minister Sadananda Biswal said,' Will it be wise if the Chief Minister will go for the campaigning of the by-election? It can be discussed later. If it is necessary, then the Chief Minister will never hesitate to go. Isn't it Mr. Bimal?'

'Yes , Sir, 'Mr. Bimalendu replied.

Sanjay Pattnaik said,' My father isn't helping me in the election campaign. I expect that printing the leaflet, banner, gate, campaign cassette, all these will be taken care of by the party. He could convey essential things in just a few minutes and felt relieved.

Ramraman said,' What's the necessity to discuss it here? The election committee of the party will help you. You have to take care of the association.'

'Also, keep an eye on your wife.' Bimalendu commented. There was a roar of laughter.

Ramraman had arranged for dinner from a five-star hotel. The menu consisted of fried rice, nan, rumali roti, mutton, chicken masala, prawn fry, palak paneer, navaratan korma, ice cream,gulab jamun.. etc. The waiters were ready to serve the dinner on the lawn. No one was interested in leaving the meeting and going for dinner without drinks. Sanjay very well knew about the likes and dislikes of the members of the party. He said, 'It's only 9O' Clock now. Why have dinner so soon? I have brought the best Scotch whiskey.'

Minister Sadananda Biswal said, 'Let's go and look at the arrangements that Sanjay has made.'

Sanjay Pattnaik had ordered for Black Label and Chivas Regal whiskey. He knew about the experienced leaders of his party. Though they speak against liquor in Vidhan Sabha, they required it for the evening party. Few people like Rajsekhar Mohanty don't consume alcohol, whereas others do. Ramaraman is the most addicted person. Once he starts drinking, it continues till midnight. His philosophy is it's right to leave the invitation of a half-naked lady but not the whisky bottle. He enjoys the whisky so much that while drinking, he forgets to have snacks.

All of them were enjoying in the dim light on the lawn. Sadananda held a glass, came near Ramraman. He sat down and said,' Why are you not taking any snacks? Raw liquor isn't good for health Ramraman babu.'

Ramraman said,' sir, I believe in keeping a balance.'

Sadananda said,' I didn't get you.'

'Sir, this earth is covered with 71% water and 29% land. How can I balance it if I don't keep the same ratio in my stomach?

Sadananda and others laughed loudly. Sanjay was pleased because they all appreciated how he hosted the party, and secondly, Ramraman forgot about his problems.

Someone commented, 'Politics is becoming difficult day by day. There is a rift at the party. Will we look after the activities of the opposition or our party?'

Sadanand could understand the intention of this comment very well. Rajsekhar Mohanty has kept all of them under his grip with the temptation of money, power, and a good position in the government. Leaders like him who have a difference of opinion in the party have appointed spy to keep an eye on them. This strategy of the ruling party was there when Mahatab was in power and is continuing. For the name's sake, it is the Republic of India, but still, Feudalism prevails. He has digested the insult and is still at the party. He will do what is needful when the time is favorable.

If the party wins in the Rourkela by-election, then Rajsekhar Mohanty will not give importance to him. It will be proved that in the western region, no one can compete with him. Sadananda was very much annoyed.

Sanjay Pattnaik was a novice in politics, but he was very good at pleasing others. How can he make an ordinary night enjoyable he knew about that very well? He made that evening so pleasant that he couldn't infer about it when he thought about it the next day. All of them appreciated Sanjay. It was only Sadananda Biswal who was feeling uncomfortable in that commotion. In the past, when he was the leader of the ruling party at that time, Sanjay Pattnaik tore his kurta and dhoti, humiliated him as a part of the conspiracy of Rajsekhar Mohanty and Ramraman, which he will never forget. Ramraman is no more in power, and till Rajsekhar becomes powerless, he will never live in peace, and for that Sanjay Pattnaik should lose the by-election.

CHAPTER-10

ROURKELA

Paluk said, 'Winter in Rourkela is too difficult. The steel plant is situated in Rourkela, and the winter is also too hard to bear.' By the time he came from Panthanivas till Basanti Colony, he was shivering.

Urbashi looked at Pulak. He was looking like a giraffe in his hooded blazer. Though Pulak was there in Delhi for a long time, still he couldn't bear the cold. He had covered himself from head to toe.

After the by-election was declared, Urbashi had come to Rourkela. As the party President made Sanjeev Ray understand, despite all his anger and huff, he supported Urbashi in all respect. Urbashi opened her office in the Basanti colony. Ghanshyam Ray, Ramprasad Kanungoo, and Kalika Ray were taking care of the election campaign, but Pulak was unofficially the election manager of Urbashi. As he was shivering in the cold, Urbashi said,' Will the people come to vote in this bitter cold?'

Pulak could understand what Urbashi meant. He ordered two cups of tea and said,' Once you go out, you won't feel cold. Am I feeling cold anymore?'

Today the party President will come for the campaigning. The election is on the 5th. Urbashi was scared as the ruling party was spending a lot of money on campaigning, but she didn't say that to Pulak. Pulak's presence has caused a raise of eyebrow among the party worker. They weren't ready to accept Pulak. The by-election is an opportunity and source to prove themselves and to earn money. They don't want an outsider to interfere and snatch that opportunity from them. Urbashi was horrified to see this attitude of the party workers. Indeed one can't win the battle with dissatisfied soldiers, but the party president interfered in this matter and solved the problem. He accepted Pulak as a member of the campaigning committee.

Urbashi and Pulak met each other very often and had respect and affection, so they were no more formal in addressing each other. There were now very close to each other.

Urbashi said,' You are looking thin. I think the weather of this place doesn't suit you.'

Pulak smiled and said,' Do you know what the problem of the human being is? He can see everything about others but can't see his condition. Look at your face in the mirror. You look like an insane lady.'

Urbashi didn't give a reply to it. The day she decided to contest the election, she only thought about the possibilities but never thought about the problems related to it. She didn't know much about the issues. During her childhood, she saw her father contesting for the Sarpanch post, and as she grew up, she saw the campaign on TV and has read the election campaign report in the newspaper. She knew that under the sheet of values and ideals, the local and personal issues impacted the election. She didn't know that she had to be careful in every step and should control her tongue. She was straightforward, so hiding her anger and keeping a smiling face was difficult for her.

In between, she has already visited the places like Panposh, Koyal Nagar, Bandamunda , Tarkera plant area, Hamirpur, and Luhakera. Her symbol in the election was 'Wheel.' She always said that the Jungle Raj of Ramraman and Sanjay would end because of this disc of optimistic vision. Every day she gives a speech in almost fourteen to fifteen election meetings. She goes in a Padyatra in the morning, and in the evening, she goes to the booth office to find the well-being of the party workers. Today was the last day of the campaign, and the distribution of the small papers had already begun. The most important thing is to keep an eye on the opposition.

Pulak kept the empty teacup on the table and got up and said Urbashi- 'You get ready. I will go and have a look at the arrangements made for the meeting in the field near Hanuman Vatika.'

Urbashi said,' sir spoke to me yesterday evening. He will come from Sambalpur and reach the circuit house situated at Panposh. Sandeep Ray had been told that a procession would take him to the field near Hanuman Vatika. Will you kindly write a speech for me today?'

Pulak said, 'There is no time to quip now. The way you can write your views, can I write similarly?'

'I am requesting you because you write much better than me.'

Urbashi's presence of mind again defeated Pulak. He

said It's ok. I will draft it, and you can include whatever you want to it.'

'Kindly include our party President's contribution for Rourkela Steel Plant, Regional Engineering College, and the township. Sir has briefed to include our party's contribution towards the development of people rather than speaking about Ramraman and Sanjay Pattnaik's corruption.

-The ruling party says that all these were done when the Prime Minister from their party was in power.

Urbashi said-' Have you not heard that there are many people who boast about success, but no one speaks about failure.'

Pulak took the responsibility of writing the speech and left. Urbashi was tired, and her legs were paining as she walked a lot. Rourkela is a big city, and people in every sector expect her to go there. The requirements of all the sectors are different. In Rourkela, the votes of the Tribals, Christians, and Muslims are more. She has to go to the temple as well as the church. Religion isn't bringing people together; instead, it's dividing people. Other than that, there are different problems in sector areas and civil areas. The people of the sector area say that the people in the civil area get all the facilities. In contrast, the people in the civil area say that they fall into the second category of the citizen in Rourkela, though they are the inhabitants of the place. The civil area is sprawling, so it's necessary to do some developmental work for them, and other than that, there are clubs in different regions, and they need cricket kits, TV, and some funds. Urbashi was surprised to see people bargaining. She didn't know about this face of politics. Indian politics is self-orientated and selfish. She shrank.

She is blessed as she has Pulak with her, and if he hadn't been there, she wouldn't have been able to do anything.

Today is an important day for her. She has to give a speech in front of the party President and other than that, she has to go to the colony where her in-laws stay for the election campaign. It is almost five years, and she has never been there. She was thrown out of the house like trash and was accused of being characterless. She gets shattered whenever she thinks about it. She still remembers the scar of the wounds on her body. Those were the wounds that healed but left a mark.

She will go to that house to ask for the vote. She knows very well that no one in that house will vote for her. She thought that she would not go to the colony where her in-laws stay as she neither wanted to invite any problem for her nor wanted to face any irreverent situation. Pulak convinced her and was able to change her decision. He put forth the argument that still Urbashi isn't able to come out of that attachment, which is why she is scared. Urbashi should remember that she is contesting in the election to be the representative of the public. Her in-laws are not different from Rourkela's general public. He quoted Goutam Buddha's example and said that Goutam Buddha first went to his wife to beg alms, and then he could free himself from all the attachments, so Urbashi must free herself from all attachments. She isn't going to her in-law's house to beg for any help. She is going to the voters to seek their support.

Urbashi remembered what Pulak said. Pulak's presence matters a lot to her, but his issues of absence to her more. Does she sometimes wonder how anyone can help others just for the sake of humanity?

It's almost six months back she met him. Pulak has never shown his inclination towards Urbashi. They are like two workers in the work field. They are different. The similarity between them is their values and ethics, and everything else is immaterial.

Pulak is always ahead of her in literature, philosophy, politics, and art. Sometimes Urbashi feels scared to speak in front of him though he is just a year senior to her studies, he has good knowledge. For the past six months, Pulak has constantly been helping her leave behind all his work. If she asks Pulak about it, he says,' Who said I have come to help you leaving behind all my work? Who will look after the showroom which we are setting up in Udit Nagar other than me? Urbashi knows that Pulak is doing all these to convince his father, but in reality, he is giving more time to Urbashi.

Yesterday advocate Sibananda Sahoo visited her. The next date of the divorce case is on 11th. The judgment for the divorce case which Sanjay Pattnaik filed will be given. If Urbashi signs in the papers, then that dispute will be solved, and it won't be necessary to wait for the court's judgment. Urbashi knowingly didn't give any reply to the advocate and sent him back. Let the election get over then she will think about the divorce case. After the results are announced on the 7th, she will decide whether to go to Cuttack or to stay in Rourkela.

Sanjay Pattnaik has hung his poster and the symbol' Lantern' in every nook and corner. They are trying their best by using Ramraman's wealth and Sanjay's power to win the election. Ramraman is scared that if they lose in the election, then the murder case in which his son is involved will again be revived, and after that, even if he tries his best, he can never influence Chief Minister Rajsekhar Mohanty.

There is a lot of discussion in Rourkela regarding the contest between the husband and wife. Sanjay Pattnaik, in his election campaign, is distributing the Xerox copy of the doctor's certificate to prove that Urbashi is insane. He is also justifying that if she wins the contest, no men can approach her as she has accused a gentleman like Ramraman of his indecent behavior. Ramraman is like Pitamaha Bhisma in Rourkela's political arena. He convinces the people to help him win the election and support Ramraman, who is in grief.

Urbashi laughed at Sanjay for his knowledge related to Mahabharata. How does Pitamaha Bhisma, who was unmarried, have a son? There is no comparison between Bhisma, who conquered the senses, and Ramraman? Ramraman and Sanjay are fiercer than thousands of Duryodhan and Dusashana. She shivered, thinking about them.

There was a gathering of the party workers in the ground floor. She has to take care of the evening meeting. The ruling party is trying to spoil the meeting. The SP, DSP, and AGM are with Ramraman, and they are not cooperating with her. Her party president is also short-tempered, and she knows it very well. During the procession, if he misbehaves someone, then at that time, there will be a tumult between the party workers and the police, and the election meeting can't be conducted. Urbashi called Sandeep Ray as the party president has told her always to consult him.

It was almost 9 a.m., but still, it was too cold and foggy. For a long time, neither the drains were cleaned nor were the roads repaired. Sector area looks neat and clean like New Delhi, whereas the civil area is dirty and looks like Old Delhi. However, she has stayed in Rourkela for so many years but has never thought about its condition. It will be wrong to say that Rourkela is a cleaner place by looking at Ring Road. The situation in the slum area is too bad. Can Urbashi change this situation?

Sometimes she gets startled. Pulak says most of the Indian politicians are like Abhimanyu. They know how to enter the maze of power, but they never think about what to do after reaching there. When they are in the opposition party, their focus is on the chair of power, but they can't assess what to do next. As a result, they enjoy the power for a few days, trouble those against them by filing CBI and vigilance cases against them, and finally start growing plump. In this way, time passes, and again it's time for the election.

Pulak says, 'It's not the time of Gandhi Ji, Nehru, or Roosevelt. Earlier, the leaders did planning and tried to involve the general public in planning and implementation, but now the leaders are following the public. During Kennedy's rule in the United States of America, public opinion surveys began, and the main objective was to understand the need of the public. In America, all the national issues are discussed, whereas, in our country, the national issues become a local issue. If the public says that a tube well will be installed, the leader will do that. If the public says a temple or a club will be constructed on the government land, the leader immediately releases funds. It was the end of the era where the public followed the leaders; now, they follow the public. A leader only thinks to become popular irrespective of whether it's giving birth to violence, superstition, and communal barrier.'

Pulak's argument was justified, but still, Urbashi had a plan in her mind for Rourkela, but she never discussed it with anyone. If she wins the election, then she will go ahead with it.

If she loses?

She gets scared to think about the answer to this question.

Pulak says, 'Defeat is a part of politics. It's not at all impossible to get defeated where foreign liquor, donation for the club, permit to encroach the government land, and religion is a technique to get votes and to win the election. But Urbashi never thought about it.

Urbashi was speaking to Sandeep Ray. She said,' I am a little nervous as they are spending so much money for the election.'

Sandeep Ray consoled her and said,' The ruling party always spends a lot of money. I have told our people to take advantage of it and keep in mind that it isn't related to whom they will vote for. Is it written in the ballot paper which the ruling party candidate is and the opposition party candidate?

Sandeep Ray is an industrialist, and he is brilliant. He can impress everyone by the way he carries himself. He is an example for others. He gets up early in the morning and finishes half of his day's work by nine in the morning.

Urbashi looked a little happy. She thanked Sandeep Ray. Sandeep Ray said,' In the afternoon around 2 p.m., we will begin the procession from Panposh's circuit house as it will take almost two hours to reach the ground near Hanuman Vatika.

The morning newspapers were scattered here and there. Urbashi had a habit of reading the newspaper from the beginning till the end, but nowadays, she hardly gets time to go through the headlines.

The reporter in Rourkela didn't create any problems for her. The newspaper 'Utkal Express' sometimes writes in favor of her and sometimes against her. Once she had asked the newspaper reporter regarding it, the reporter said that it's the neutral aspect of their newspaper. Urbashi couldn't give a reply to this. She wasn't so much interested in journalism, reporters, and the newspaper.

In between Bharat Mahapatra had contacted her twice from Bhubaneswar. He told her that her interview in 'OSF India' was appreciated by many. Urbashi utilized him to get a ticket for the election, and she was grateful towards him. In the beginning, Bharat Mahapatra's attitude towards her wasn't that good, but now she could realize that there is a lot of change in his attitude. Bharat Mahapatra was the reporter who reported about Urbashi getting the opposition party's ticket, which has enhanced his reputation. If Urbashi wins the election and goes to the capital, she will meet him to show her gratefulness.

Pulak also informed her that the exclusive interview of Bharat Mahapatra with her was read by many. She was congratulated by many from other states. An institution from Bhopal appreciated the courage of Urbashi and wrote an appreciation letter. Her party President isn't influenced by this type of news in the newspaper; rather, he says this doesn't control eighty percent of voters. Newspaper, radio, and TV have importance for only twenty percent of people who live in the cities. So it's not necessary to focus on this; rather, efforts should be made to reach the commoner. Urbashi was about to enter the washroom when Ramesh brought the cordless, gave it to her, and said,' It's urgent. Someone has called you.'

Urbashi took the call and said,' Urbashi here.'

'Do you remember about Monalisa Dutta?'

'Who is Monalisa?'

'Monalisa who's hysterectomy-'

Urbashi was surprised. She said,' Yes, yes. I remember it very well. I have never forgotten her. Where did she go, and who are you?'

'I was told by the minister Mr. Sadananda Biswal to give you the information. Can you arrange for an interview with Monalisa along with the newspaper reporter? I will give you her Kolkata address.'

Urbashi said with enthusiasm,' Yes, yes.'

'He said as you have never seen her. How will you recognize her?'

'I will make the necessary arrangements. If I can get a photograph of her, then I can give it to the reporter.'

'Sir told me to give you the information. I will speak to you later.' He disconnected the call. There was a lot of excitement in Urbashi. It was the excitement of getting an invincible weapon.

How will she get the photograph of Monalisa? She

suddenly remembered that her co-sister could help her in this matter. She will go there for the election campaign. Urbashi made her plans.

Next is the interview. Maybe the newspaper reporters may not cooperate with her. 'Utkal Express' neutral newspaper may help her out, but they may take it differently. Can the reporter Bharat Mahapatra help her in this regard? Her party President is the only person who can tell him to do so because he may not listen to Urbashi. If an interview with Monalisa's photograph can be printed and distributed in Rourkela, then people will come to know about the reality of Ramraman and Sanjay Pattnaik.

How will Sadananda Biswal benefit from this? Arabs asked Pulak.

Pulak said, 'In the school of politics, you are still a new admit, so you can't understand the nuances of politics.' He also made her understand the rivalry between Rajsekhar and Sadananda. Pulak also said,' The Chief Minister commented that Sadananda is like a night watchman. Sadananda can never forget his comment. So we should give importance to Sadananda's proposal.'

-Kindly think over the questions to be asked to Monalisa. I will speak to you after an hour.

- Pulak said-'Yes' and disconnected the call.

Urbashi was much excited.

CHAPTER -11

THE CAPITAL

N ight Watchman! Sadananda Biswal could never forget this sarcastic comment. At that time, as the party High Command interfered, Rajsekhar Mohanty had to quit from his seat and became the Chief Minister. After three months, the election was held, and his party lost. If his party won, he would have taken the oath as the Chief Minister for the second time, but it couldn't happen. Rajsekhar Mohanty's internal politics, black money, the display of political power, and the corrupted regime brought disgrace to the ruling party. They gave a chance to the opposition party to take over the command easily. Rajsekhar Mohanty blamed him for the Defeat and commented that he couldn't manage the election properly.

Many of them are defeated by Rajsekhar Mohanty's dirty politics. He was the representative of the backward class so that he couldn't prosper so quickly. Despite all these, he hoped that his candidature would be considered and he would become the Chief Minister. He discussed this with the party supervisor before the election, but he was again circumvented. He came to know that Rajsekhar Mohanty had written an application regarding the central grant and had taken the signature of the MLAs in that, but later on, this content changed. In the edited application, though the signatures were there, the subject matter of the application changed. The point in the application was- they support the candidature of Rajsekhar Mohanty as the Chief Minister. After listening to this Sadananda Biswal's blood pressure increased, and he was admitted to the hospital. Rajsekhar Mohanty didn't miss this chance to play dirty politics. He visited him in the hospital and announced that Sadananda Biswal, the party's senior leader, is unwell. The reason behind this announcement was to make it clear that important and difficult work shouldn't be assigned to him.

Sadananda wanted to go for the campaigning of the Rourkela's by-election, but a planning committee meeting was called, and he wasn't allowed to go. Though he came to know about this plan, he couldn't do anything.

He doesn't have any rivalry with Ramraman. Though Ramraman is a follower of Rajsekhar, he doesn't oppose him. If the party member wins the by-election, then Rajsekhar will not obey anyone. He will again be an essential and respectable person in front of the Delhi High Command. Ramraman wasn't only an MLA but also was a minister. According to the rule, someone should be the minister from Sundergard district, and if by chance Sanjay Pattnaik becomes the minister, then it will create a big problem. It may happen that he will be thrown out from the ministry after the by-election as in the eighties, The chief minister had taken the Revenue Department away from him. So Sanjay Pattnaik must lose.

An interview with Monalisa, who was the kept of Ramraman, will have an impact. It would have been good if it had been printed earlier. Still, Sadananda didn't do it purposely because the candidate would have got a chance to give explanations regarding the issue rather this last moment assail will be more fruitful.

Minister Sadananda told his associate to call Bharat Mahapatra. He called him.

-Mr. Bharat. Is that you?

- Sir, sir. Reporter Bharat Mahapatra said in a soft voice.

- You are the kingmaker now. Why will you think about us now? Sadananda said mockingly.

Bharat said-' I wanted to meet you, but I couldn't.'

Sadananda said mockingly,' Oh! Is it so that you couldn't meet me?' Then he asked him,' What is your opinion about Rourkela's by-election?'

Sir, I can't predict anything about it. Sanjay Pattnaik and Ramraman are too powerful.

Then will you get defeated?

Sir, I can't understand what do you mean?

All of them are saying that Urbashi is your candidate and if she is defeated, won't it be your Defeat?

Bharat Mahapatra giggled and said,' You mock differently. You are too sharp.'

Sadananda said in a firm voice,' There is something important to discuss with you. You may come to the guest house in the evening. We will discuss it there.'

Bharat Mahapatra showed his approval.

Sadananda kept the phone down, smiled, and said,

now a day's words have wings. It's not wise to speak in detail over the phone.

He lit a cigarette. In the western region, his party is very powerful. He has already started the groundwork there. After the by-election, he will visit Delhi. He will inform the high command that it will be challenging to win the upcoming Vidhan Sabha election if the party leadership isn't changed. His party will completely uproot the ruling party. If it happens, then, he along with his twenty-seven supporters will join the opposition party. It doesn't matter if he doesn't become the Chief Minister, but no one can stop him from becoming the Deputy Chief Minister. There are fifty-seven members in the opposition party, and in the Communist, Jharkhand, and other parties, there are ten members each. So if all of them join together, there will be eighty-seven members. Rajsekhar Mohanty has manipulated and has become the Chief Minister, and now he will also play the same trick with him to bring him down from the seat.

Minister Sadananda belonged to an impoverished family. He didn't get a chance to pursue his studies properly during his childhood, and with a lot of difficulties, he completed his Intermediate. Keeping this in view, Rajsekhar Mohanty has continually ignored his candidature as he is highly qualified. He has a double doctorate and is also a well-known writer.

It's enough now to tolerate. Sadananda thought and extinguished the burning cigarette as if it's not a piece of the cigarette but Rajsekhar Mohanty's Chief Ministership.

When Sadananda was sitting in his office and was thinking about it, Ramraman Sarangi was in his government quarters and was speaking to Sanjay Pattnaik over the phone. Sanjay Pattnaik was speaking in an agitated voice,' If CM doesn't come by helicopter again, then it's sure that we will lose. You try to bring him here. Today is the campaign's last day, and if CM doesn't come, then things will be worse.'

Ramraman was able to convince the Chief Minister. He would have been to Rourkela in a private helicopter, but at the last moment, he canceled the program. The Chief Minister couldn't visit Rourkela.

Minister Sadananda said that if the Chief Minister visits very often to campaign for the by-election, then it will have an adverse effect, and there will be a notion that the local affiliate is weak and other than that if after the second visit of the Chief Minister the party loses then that will be projected as faithlessness. The Chief Minister is the state's leader, and the ruling party's existence depends on his image, so the Chief Minister shouldn't go for campaigning anymore.

Ramraman couldn't understand whether it was because of Sadananda's resistance or any other reason why the Chief Minister canceled the plan. He knew well about the difference in opinion between the Chief Minister and Sadananda. So how could the Chief Minister listen to him and cancel his trip? He couldn't believe it. Then what can be the reason?

Sanjay Pattnaik was screaming in helplessness. He said that he would commit suicide or withdraw from the election. Ramraman said,' Don't worry about the helicopter. I will take the aircraft and go. I will go and meet the CM and try to take him along with me. Despite that, if the CM isn't able to go, there is nothing to worry about. Think that we have won the election. No one can stop us from winning the election.'

After listening to this Sanjay Pattnaik became a little cool. He said,' That's ok, but if the Chief Minister would have come here once....'

Do whatever I have told you. During the meeting, those things should be gifted on the stage. Remember that you aren't going to send anyone who is known to you. You have to send unknown people.

Sanjay said,' Yes, sir.'

-Keep in mind that not many people should be able to go to their meeting. The road construction work is going on near the fertilizer plant. Make some arrangements so that there will be a traffic jam for almost two hours.

- I have already made the necessary arrangements. Our people are ready. If there can be one round of blank fire, it will be good as the tribal people will be scared and run away.

- 'It's ok. We will discuss it when I reach there tomorrow.'

Ramraman kept the phone down. He has to leave for Rourkela the next day. In between the election campaign, he never wanted to come to Bhubaneswar, but he had faith that maybe the Chief Minister would agree to go with him, so he came, but his arrival at Bhubaneswar didn't go in vain could arrange funds for the party.

He leaned on the sofa. He isn't going to be in a problem if Sanjay Pattnaik wins or loses. If he wins, then

Ramraman will say that he won for him, and if he loses, it will be said that he lost only because of his political image. Of course, if he wins, he will benefit as the man can do anything required, and he is useful to him.

Ramraman was a little upset as there was a change in the political scenario. He never expected that such a situation would arise. Now he has got used to it. He requested the Chief Minister for the last time as it was the correct time to meet him. If he can meet him, he will most likely be able to convince him and take him to Rourkela the following day.

CHAPTER 12

ROURKELA

The ground near the Hanuman Vatika was crowded. During the sixties, when the President of the opposition party was the right hand of Mahatab at that time, the Rourkela Steel plant was constructed. In the year 1961, the Chief Minister was the President of the party, and at that time, the Engineering College was established in Rourkela. The people of the city had faith and belief in him.

The President said Urbashi,' You can't evaluate your popularity by looking at the crowd. They have a role to play. I get a lot of love and affection from the people of Rourkela and Paradeep.

Urbashi knows how this leader took a bold decision to construct the port in Paradeep, how he had given the instructions to build the highway from Daitari till Paradeep. When Urbashi was accompanying him to Delhi on the flight, she asked him,' Even though your party is so popular, why does it get defeated?'

He remained quiet for some time and said,' I am short-tempered and impatient, and these are my enemies. Other than that, there is a lot of jealousy and blame game in Odisha.'

Sandeep Ray was giving his welcome speech on the ground near Hanuman Vatika, followed by Urbashi's and the President's speech. Urbashi opened her vanity bag and checked if the speech which Pulak had written was there or not. Pulak was sitting behind the party President, and he was excited.

A young man who was well dressed with a thick gold chain on his neck with golden frame spectacles and looked like an elite businessman climbed the stage with a gift packet. A red ribbon was tied to the pack. Urbashi couldn't recognize the man. Sandeep Ray stopped delivering his speech in between and asked, 'What's the matter?' The man greeted everyone and then kept the packet in front of the party President and went away. Urbashi looked at the man for some time, but after that, she couldn't see him.

The party President instructed them to take the packet away to a distant place and to open it. Urbashi was frightened. Can it be a bomb? How did the police allow this man to climb the stage?

There wasn't a bomb in the packet, but something was not less than explosive. There was a torn blouse, a condom packet, a rope, and a mopping cloth. Sanjay Pattnaik had sent those to Urbashi. The party President was astonished to see those things. What does it mean?

A few young men shouted at the top of their voices that these things would be helpful for madam in the meeting. Could you give it to her? If she needs more, then we will send her.

Sandeep Ray's speech wasn't yet over. There was chaos in the meeting, and no one could hear what he was saying. He stopped delivering his speech and sat down.

Urbashi looked at the party President and Pulak.

She took the microphone in her hand and stood up, but she didn't go near the podium and said in a loud voice-' All these things will be beneficial for me.' The chaos in the meeting slowly settled down. Urbashi was draped in a white saree with a blue border, and her voice was crystal clear. She wiped the sweat on her forehead and began her speech. She said,' Do you know why Sanjay Pattnaik has sent this torn blouse, condom, a rope, and a mopping cloth? You may not know, but I know the reason. I am insane, so this rope should tie me, as I am destitute to earn my living by mopping others' houses. I am a characterless prostitute so that I will keep condoms for my customers, and if again I go against Sanjay Pattnaik he will make my condition like this torn blouse. My dear brothers and sisters, I wanted to say something about Rourkela and for the people of Rourkela, but it will be unfair if I don't give a reply to Ramraman and Sanjay Pattanik as all of you may misunderstand me.'

'Sanjay Pattnaik also should know that a woman taught Adi Guru Sankaracharya about Kamasutra. In Indian tradition, an unmarried girl is worshipped as there is a notion that Devi Laxmi dwells in her. During the oblation, if a woman doesn't sit with a man, the ritual isn't complete. How can a man like Sanjay Pattnaik have been born if a woman wouldn't have been there?

Suddenly the meeting place reverberated with claps. Those who had seen Urbashi before were captivated by her speech, and her personality and impressive speech enchanted those who didn't see her before.

Urbashi said, 'I will keep this gift carefully till I am alive as Draupadi kept her hair open. Though I want to forget Sanjay Pattnaik will never let me forget. The public will decide whether they will elect me as their representative or Sanjay Pattnaik, who got an unmarried girl operated and took out her uterus, wanted a divorce from his wife by producing a false certificate that she is insane; took away a child from her mother. Sanjay Pattnaik has won in every game of life, but I hope that the people of Rourkela will help me to win the election and make my life fruitful.'

The meeting place again reverberated with continuous clapping.

Urbashi Pattnaik Zindabad!

Opposition party President Zindabad!

Ramraman Murdabad!

Let us vote for the wheel symbol.

Urbashi kept the microphone in front of the party President and sat down. She was neither crying nor laughing, nor was she happy. She was firm.

The party President stood up to give the speech. He spoke a line,' Insane, characterless, short-tempered- doesn't matter what you say, Urbashi is my daughter. She is the most suitable heir of mine. I have let her contest this election and to help her to win is your responsibility.'

Urbashi went and stood near the party President. He held her hand high, and the ground reverberated with the clapping sound.

CHAPTER 13

ROURKELA

It was almost late at night, and Urbashi woke up when she heard someone banging the door. She switched on the light and looked at the wall clock. It was almost 1 a.m. Who is there so late at night?

She asked,' Who is that?'

'Open the door. I am Pulak.'

Urbashi was startled. Why is Pulak here so late at night? There must be some problem.

Pulak was staying in Panthanivas, and after two days, he will return to the capital. Till 11 O'Clock, all of them were on the ground floor of the house. The next day is the election. It was planned that at 7.30 a.m., she would go with Sandeep Ray to the Udit Nagar booth to cast her vote, and as Pulak doesn't have his name in Rourkela's voter list, he will go to Koel Nagar and keep an eye on the booths.

There was again banging at the door.

Urbashi arranged her saree and came out. She covered herself with a shawl and went near the door and said,' Wait, let me open the door.'

As soon as she opened the door, Pulak held her hand

and dragged her. By the time she could ask him anything, he had already taken her downstairs. In front of the party office, he had parked his vehicle. He said,' Sit down quickly, and he started the car.'

They are near Chand colony. Urbashi asked,' What happened?' Why are you taking me like this at midnight as if you are kidnapping me? What's your motive?'

He said,' We have to hide somewhere for a few hours. Ramraman and Sanjay Pattnaik's ruffians may attack your house anytime.'

Though it was biting cold outside, Urbashi started sweating. It's not impossible for Ramraman and Sanjay Pattnaik. How did Pulak get this information? The police are also along with Ramraman and Sanjay Pattnaik.

The light of the Maruti car was glowing in the darkness of Rourkela's ring road. There was silence everywhere. There is a difference between the city in the daytime and at night. The orange light of the traffic was blinking.

-Where will we go?

- I am thinking about it. Whom will we wake up so late at night?

- Shall we go to your room in Panthanivas?

- I think you don't have brains. If they don't find you in Basanti Colony, then they will go to Panthanivas.

- Let's go to Udit Nagar police station.

- I can't trust anyone here. All are dangerous.

A police jeep was seen coming towards them. Pulak

turned the car towards IGH Hospital. He said,' Let me see if Dr. Mahapatra is there or not.'

-What will you do if he is there? Are we going to get admitted to the hospital?

- No, we will take his car and go. They can recognize my car so that we will keep it here. No one will suspect us as many people come to the hospital. You cover yourself and sit in the car. I will come back immediately. Pulak covered his face with the monkey cap. Many people in Rourkela do not know him. With his appearance and the way he speaks, no one can make out whether he belongs to Odisha. He speaks partly in Hindi and partly in English, but he is very good at writing the Odiya language.

Pulak came back after fifteen minutes. He said, 'Come, let's take Dr. Mahapatra's car and go. Let our car be here.'

Did you say that I am with you?

Pulak looked here and there and said,' No one is there with me.'

Urabashi understood what Pulak meant. Though it was cold, still she was sweating. She went and sat in Dr. Mahapatra's car, and Pulak drove it.

It was a long wintery night.

Dr. Mahapatra's car had the doctor's symbol in the front and back so no one would suspect. At midnight on the roads of Rourkela, the police vehicles and doctor's vehicles ply.

Urbashi said,' Let's go to the station and sit on the platform for some time.

Pulak refused and said, 'It's not wise to take any risk. Let's go to the church which is in Sector 9.'

Urbashi said, 'Take me wherever you want. You are now my charioteer.'

Pulak drove the car towards the church.

Urbashi was staring at Pulak, and as she looked at him, she was attracted towards him. It was a strange feeling. A person in whose life people like Sanjay Pattnaik was there in her life Pulak is also there. The irony is the person who was supposed to come into her life first came later, and the person who came into her life first destroyed her life.

The atmosphere was foggy, and the wind was chill.

Pulak said, 'You will remember this night as the longest night in your life.'

Urbashi asked,' How did you know that they would come and attack me? How will this benefit them?'

Pulak said coolly,' If you die, then there won't be any election tomorrow.'

Urbashi was stunned. She said, 'We could have asked for the police protection. I told that to Mr. Sandeep Ray.'

Pulak said, 'Rourkela police will never help us till Ramraman is in power.' Pulak said,' The interview of Monalisa Dutta has perturbed them because they doubt that you have stolen the photo from Sanjay Pattnaik's house.'

'What suspect? It's true.' Urbashi said

'Where was that photo, and who told you that? Are there enemies of Ravan in Lanka too?'

Urbashi said,' I will disclose the name later on. Tell me who gave you the information about the attack?'

'People of minister Sadananda Biswal.'

Urabashi kept quiet as she knew that if the information had come from Sadanada Biswal, it's hundred percent correct. She was scared as she understood the gravity of the situation. Pulak could understand it from her expression. He consoled Urbashi and said,' In your life, you have fought many times with death. How can you be scared?'

She felt a little comfortable. The dawn was nearing. Both of them were sitting on the porch and looking at the sky. Who knows where fate will take them. It doesn't matter if she wins or loses. Urvashi's life will not be like it was before. Pulak has to go back to the capital.

Urbashi asked,' Pulak, will you remember this night?'

Pulak replied,' Yes, forever.'

- 'What name will I give to the relation that I have with you?'

Pulak said,' Urbashi when the relationship is given a name, then its value diminishes. Suppose it's named as a friend, husband, lover, son, or brother that arbitrarily confines the relationships in the narrow lanes of those words. A relationship exists beyond this. It will be better if you don't try to give a name to this relationship.'

Urbashi said,' Pulak, you must have read what Shri Krishna said to Arjuna after showing his Universal Form(Vishvarupa).'

Pulak wanted to make the situation lighter and said,'
I don't read Gita or Bhagawat.'

Urbashi said,' You are lying to me.'

Pulak took out his gloves, stood up, and said,' Say,
what you want to say.'

In the backdrop, there was the church, above was the
sky, and below was the earth. Urbashi opened the car door,
came out, and chanted the slokas from Gita in her fantastic
voice.

> sakheti matvā prasabham yad uktam
> he kriṣhṇa he yādava he sakheti
> ajānatā mahimānam tavedam
> mayā pramādāt praṇayena vāpi
> yach chāvahāsārtham asat-kṛito 'si
> vihāra-śhayyāsana-bhojaneṣhu
> eko 'tha vāpy achyuta tat-samakṣham
> tat kṣhāmaye tvām aham aprameyam

Pulak explained,' Thinking of you as my friend, I
presumptuously addressed you as, "O Krishna," "O Yadav,"
"O my dear mate." I was ignorant of your majesty, showing
negligence and undue affection. And if, jestfully, I treated
you with disrespect, while playing, resting, sitting, eating,
when alone, or before others—for all that I crave forgiveness.'

Urbashi was, listening to the explanation of Pulak.
A while ago, the night that seemed dark, calm, and long
was now bright, warm, and short. Urbashi thought that the
night should be longer than ever, let it be darker, but Pulak
should be there with her. If there is a company, no night
will be longer, and no road will be endless.

Both of them sat quietly. After a while, Pulak called Urbashi, who was engrossed in her thoughts. She was startled.

Pulak said,' Look! Urbashi.'

Urbashi looked towards the East. The sun was rising through the darkness. One could hear the chirping of the birds.

Pulak said,' Let's go.'

They weren't returning to Basanti colony but going to Panthanivas as they knew their party office in Basanti colony might have been ransacked

CHAPTER 14

ROURKELA

All India Radio's morning local news-The result of Rourkela's by-election has already been declared. Urbashi Pattnaik has defeated her opponent Sanjay Pattnaik of the ruling party by fifty thousand votes and was elected.

By 4 p.m., the counting of votes was over, but the result was officially declared at 5 p.m. Pulak was present in the vote-counting centre from the morning till evening at 4 p.m. In the afternoon, Urbashi was leading. Around 2 p.m., there was a phone call from the party President. He said,' I knew from the beginning that you would win because you convinced me and took the ticket. Congratulations! Dear Girl. One day you will become the minister and after you get the certificate from the ADM, call me.'

Urbashi couldn't give a reply as her throat was choked with tears and emotion. She had no words to thank the gentleman. If he wouldn't have given her a ticket on that day, then she would have spent her days in the Working Women's Hostel in Cuttack, and after that, who knows where her fate would have taken her? Of late, Urbashi had never cried in sadness or happiness. After she became a contestant in the election, she didn't get time to think about it. She was hurtling and today is the end of the chase, which made her emotional, but there is a difference in the situation. There was a time when there were tears of pain, and now it is the tears of happiness in her eyes.

In the evening, there was a procession of their victory. Sandeep Ray had decorated an open jeep with flowers. There was a prominent wheel symbol in front of the jeep. The parade started from Panposh and ended near the Jagganath temple of Koel Nagar. Urbashi went around the city in that procession. On the way, many party workers, thousands of people, children, and senior citizens stood to congratulate her on her victory. Sometimes in between the procession, they halted. Sandeep Ray, during the parade, told her,' It was Ramraman for whom Sanjay Pattnaik was defeated. He thought himself to be very clever, and this is the consequence of that. Their plan to attack you was like a boomerang for them, and other than that, the interview of Monalisa Dutta was killing.'

Urbashi didn't give any reply. Many people had helped her in this election. Minister Sadananda Biswal, the reporters of the newspaper 'Utkal Express and 'OSF India' and many intellectual people of Rourkela, had helped her directly or indirectly. She can never repay them.

CHAPTER-15

ROURKELA

By the time the procession and the dinner were over, it was too late. Urbashi was tired, but she had to go to Bhubaneswar. She has to finish her work at Bhubaneswar and return to Rourkela by the 10th.

She opened all the doors and windows, and the rays of the sun fell on her bed. She loved the warmth of the sunray on a wintery morning. Urbashi sat on the sofa. She couldn't understand why she was sad. Till yesterday, winning the election was her prime goal, and today after she won, she had the same feeling of a soldier after the war.

There were many gifts scattered around in the drawing-room, but there is a vacuum in all those things. She felt lonely without a companion.

She doesn't have anyone with her on whose shoulder she could lean on, share her feelings. She felt too tired and exhausted standing alone in the path of life.

She remembered about Nilamadhaba. Where did he vanish like the fog of a wintery morning? If she had met him once, Urbashi would have asked him,' Does anyone leave like this in the midway?'

Someone rang the doorbell. After some time the

place will be crowded. People who were against her would act as if they were with her. In these six months, she has understood the characteristics of human beings.

She called Malati and said,' Check who has come. I am unable to walk.'

Malati brought a cup of tea for her and said,' A lady along with her ten to eleven years old daughter has come to meet you.'

Urbashi was surprised. Who are they -who? Why did they come so early in the morning? She kept the cup on the table and went downstairs. The house was dirty with leaflets, empty glasses, empty water bottles, and withered flowers scattered all around. It will take a lot of time to clean.

A lady, along with her daughter, was sitting with their back towards the staircase. Urbashi was walking down slowly, wrapping her shawl. She was tired. As soon as the lady looked at her, Urbashi ran towards her and embraced her, and said,' Why did you come, sister? You could have informed me.'

Her co-sister had come to meet her. She said, 'Look at her.' Urbashi was extremely happy. Her daughter Miki was standing in front of her. She hugged Miki tightly. Her co-sister couldn't stop herself from crying after looking at them. She wiped her tears. Malati was standing and looking at them.

Urbashi was holding Miki tightly and was asking her,' Do you remember me, Miki? You were too small when I left your house.'

Miki didn't speak anything and was looking at her. She felt the warmth of her mother and was holding her tightly as if she would never leave her. Her co-sister said,' At home, all of them are repenting for their wrong deeds. Will you not forgive them?'

'No,' someone said firmly.

Who said this? Urbashi, her co-sister, and her daughter were startled. They looked at the door and saw Pulak standing there. He was listening to their conversation.

Pulak entered the room and said to Urbashi's co-sister,' Greetings, Madam. Kindly understand me, but today, Urbashi can't take any decision alone. Once upon a time, she had that opportunity but not now.'

Urbashi said, 'Sister, you may go now. I have been used as a swing by them for many years, but not anymore. I have left that place long back, and I can't return there again.'

Urbashi again hugged Miki, standing there, and said,' On 11th, there is a hearing of the case, and the judgment will be given. Once you have been told that you will stay with your father and on the 11th, you will decide with whom you will stay. But Miki, remember one thing that you are also a girl like your mother. You may go as I don't want to keep you here without informing anyone.'

Her co-sister and Miki left. She ran towards the door and looked at them. Miki was strolling, and her co-sister was holding her hand. Maybe she was wiping her tears.

Urbashi couldn't control her tears. After some time, Pulak said,' I think you will take some time to get ready.

I heard a piece of important news. Minister Sadananda Biswal, along with his supporters, may join our party. If that happens, there will be many changes, and maybe this government will fall. I will leave for Bhubaneswar and will meet you there.' He was going away in a hurry, and Urbashi called him and said,' Wait.'

Pulak was startled and turned back. The plastic folder which he was holding fell and the papers scattered here and there. Urbashi bent down to help Pulak. She was surprised when she saw an invitation card among those papers. She asked,' Where did you get this invitation card?'

Pulak was silent, as if he didn't want to answer her question. Urbashi asked in a louder voice,' Tell me, Pulak, how did you get the invitation card I sent to Nilamadhab? Where is Nilamadhaba? Where is he?'

Pulak said softly, 'Think that Nilamadhaba wasn't there. He was never there.'

'You are lying to me. Nilamadhaba was there, and he is there.'

'Kindly believe me. Nilamadhaba isn't there.'

'How can I believe you?'

'Because I have burnt his dead body myself.'

Urbashi was disheartened. Both of them remained silent for some time.

Pulak said,' Nilamadhaba had brain cancer. His parents tried their best to save him but couldn't succeed. When your marriage invitation card reached him, he was struggling between life and death in the hospital. Before he died, he gave me the collection of his poetry and this invitation card. He loved you deeply and spoke about you for hours. If he had recovered, he would have come back to Odisha to meet you, but that couldn't happen. After I returned from Delhi, I wanted to tell you everything, but your address had changed by that time. I thought you must be happy with your family, but I learned about your ill-fate after reading a feature. I feel ashamed that I couldn't help you when you required it the most. You had to fight your battle alone.'

Urbashi was holding the old invitation card as if it was not a piece of paper but Nilamadahaba. She never expected to hear a sample of bad news on the first day of her happiness.

She sat down. Pulak said,' Urbashi, please get up. You have to go to Bhubaneswar immediately. You must be there as the situation in the capital is different. You can't reach there before eight hours.'

Urbashi wasn't able to hear anything. She cried bitterly.

Pulak went near her to console her.

Urbashi said,' Why will I go to Bhubaneswar? Pulak, I have lost everything.'

Pulak held Urbashi's hand and made her stand. He took her near the window and opened the curtains, and said,' Look Urbashi! This is your Rourkela, where lakhs of people have voted for you to win and become their representative. Maybe they have a Urbashi, a Monalisa, or a Miki who are alive with their fate in their house. Like your mother, many helpless mothers might be there with tears in their eyes. Listen to them. Go to them. Why are you saying that you have lost everything? You are an MLA now, and tomorrow you may become a minister. You will be the person to help lakhs of people. Begin your life from here.'

Urbashi looked at Pulak. Like other days the same expression of commitment was reflecting on his face. She couldn't speak anything. A new life was waiting for her.

■

Black Eagle Books

www.blackeaglebooks.org
info@blackeaglebooks.org

Black Eagle Books, an independent publisher, was founded
as a nonprofit organization in April, 2019. It is our mission
to connect and engage the Indian diaspora and the world at
large with the best of works of world literature published
on a collaborative platform, with special emphasis on
foregrounding Contemporary Classics and New Writing.